THE AEROWYN TALES

Bellarose
AND THE
Beast

CARLA REIGHARD

For anyone who is bold enough to read fairy tales and brave enough to believe in redemption.
"Some day you will be old enough to start reading fairy tales again." ~
C.S. Lewis

Acknowledgements

Thank you, Megan Wors from @JustLikeGilmoreGirls for inspiring this whole series. You asked for a Gaston story that led my imagination to this wild adventure—*The Aerowyn Tales*.

Thank you to my beta readers: Jenn Phares, Renee Knight, and Marlena Smith. You definitely found those nasty errors that courageously escaped detection after a million reads.

Cathy McCrumb, Thank you for editing this book. I was blessed to have met you on social media as you gave my story the exact help it needed.

Benita Thompson, your cover design is perfect for this story. Thank you!

Chapter 1

Bellarose

Who enjoys reading a riches to rags story? I don't. Bellarose Bonnay—Bella for short—thought as she stared down at the drained, winterized pool. She lowered herself onto the cold concrete and crossed her legs at the edge of the gray, protective tarp. Her new dismal surroundings reminded Bella that even though she loved books for escape, her own life story wouldn't be one she'd enjoy reading.

Her thick green sweater was all she needed for the unseasonably tepid Colorado December temperatures. She missed the normal blanket of snow that may have livened up the drab surroundings. Bella had planned on taking advantage of the good weather and read outside, but the hard, chilly surface added to her misery and distracted thoughts. Still, she wanted anything to escape from her new reality and the rundown meagerly furnished apartment.

Instead of a retreat, however, stale cigarette odors wafted from nearby ashtrays—another thing that cemented the truth of her dismal circumstances. The "castle" in the name Castle Creek Apartments promised luxury, but the complex was anything but luxurious.

The small two-bedroom apartment was stifling and there was nowhere else to go to enjoy her favorite past time. Bella turned another page, but she couldn't concentrate on *A Christmas Carol*. Not even her annual December favorite could drag her away from the surroundings and its lack of Christmas cheer; the reminders of her miserable new life.

She wanted to be grateful her family wasn't homeless, but it was easier to focus on the negatives in her current state of mind. Her favorite stories were normally an escape to help move past the pity party, but she kept rereading the same sentence multiple times.

"You must be the new girl."

Bella's wandering attention jerked up to see a girl who seemed close to her own age near the gate. The girl's pretty blonde hair reminded Bella of her former friends' salon-maintained color, but the resemblance stopped there. Her friends would have mocked the worn unbranded boots and jeans this girl wore. That part, the shallow materialism, of her old life, Bella didn't miss. That was one more thing to be thankful for.

The other teen flashed perfectly straight white teeth. "I'm Elayne, but I like to be called Layney." She sat down beside Bella and crossed her legs to sit at the edge of the pool too.

Bella scooted over to avoid touching this girl who was invading her personal space.

"What's your name?"

"I'm Bellarose." She paused, and then added, "You can call me Bella."

Layney's blue eyes brightened. "Bella. That's pretty."

"Yeah, my parents wanted the French word for 'beautiful' because Mom got pregnant with me when they went to Paris. Since roses are my mom's favorite flowers, she added the rose to it."

Bella bit her lip. She didn't know anything about this girl except her name.

"'Beautiful rose'? That's cool!" Layney's smile grew. "It sounds like something from a book." She nudged Bella's arm. "You like to read?"

Books were a safer topic, and Bella relaxed. "I really do. What about you?"

"I love books!" What's that you're reading?"

Bella closed the book to show Layney the cover.

"*A Christmas Carol*—Is that about those ghosts? I think I saw a movie about it, but I haven't read that one yet." Layney paused as if anticipating a response from Bella, then continued, "Since you're new I could show you around unless you already know this part of town."

"I don't." Bella didn't want to get into the details, but she knew she needed to make new friends after her old ones ditched her.

"Where did you live before?"

Bella heaved out a huge breath. "It's a mess."

Layney leaned back on her hands and studied Bella. "It's alright, you know. We're all a bit of a mess here."

For a moment, Bella wanted to build a wall and block Layney from seeing her heart. She was still hurting from her friends' betrayal. But that was the problem. Bella no longer had any friends. After her supposed friends learned that she wouldn't be attending the elite private school, they ignored her texts and calls. The sting of that rejection made Bella want to be sucked into a fantasy book world—never to return to reality.

Bella drew a deep breath. She may not want to accept this new situation, but being lonely and friendless would only make everything worse. Was she desperate enough for friendship that she would risk trusting this girl who was a little bit sketchy? Friendship was built over time and Layney was acting like they had already shared many experiences together. She didn't have to be completely transparent, but then you get what you give.

Bella dropped her walls and let the words tumble out quickly. "My dad lost his job a few days ago." She faced Layney. "The bank foreclosed on our house. We lost everything. Basically, all I have left of my old life are my books, a bike, and some of my clothes."

"I'm sorry." Layney frowned empathetically.

"You didn't do it. You have nothing to be sorry about." Bella was relieved Layney didn't criticize or reject her.

"I didn't mean that kind of sorry." Layney paused. "I meant that it sucks, and I feel sorry for you. Not in a pathetic-loser kind of way," she added hastily. "I don't want to make you feel bad. I meant it in a I'm-here-if-you-need-a-friend kind of way."

Bella almost smiled. Layney talked like an audiobook on the fastest speed. There was relief in the fact that Layney hadn't ditched her after hearing the uncomfortable truth. Perhaps that alone was a reason to trust this stranger.

Bella paused and looked into Layney's eyes. "I had to leave my former school, Delacour Academy and my friends—or should I say *former* friends? They ghosted me when they found out I was poor."

Bella slouched and tears threatened to escape, but she swallowed hard to keep them at bay.

"Ouch." Layney winced. "They don't sound like real friends at all. But, at least you know? Anyway, it's Christmas break? We don't start back up for a while. Maybe you can read a ton of books or meet some people who will be going to your new school. Will you be going to Eastlake High?"

Bella hugged the book tighter. "I think so. What a way to finish my year."

"What grade are you in?" Layney asked.

"Twelfth."

Layney bopped up and down. "I'm a senior, too! Really, though Eastlake isn't bad. A few of the guys who live here go there. A couple are in our class." Layney softened her tone. "Since you shared some of your life story with me, I thought I would give you some of mine. It is the reason I live here. My mom died when I was a baby."

"Now it's my turn to say I'm sorry even though it's not my fault."

As Bella had thought earlier, *you get what you give*. She had shared more than she would have with this stranger and in return Layney opened Bella's eyes to the fact that Layney understood loss too.

Layney gave a half-smile. "It's okay. I didn't know my mom to miss her, but it's hard not having her around for the special stuff moms and daughters normally share. At least my dad moved us in with his aunt and she became somewhat of a mother to me. When I was too little to do things for myself, she was able to care for me when Dad was at work."

"That's rough. It's hard growing up not being able to do things with your mother and now you're stuck here." At least Bella's parents were alive and she felt ashamed about her pity party.

"It's all I've known, but I didn't tell you so you'd feel sorry for me." Layney sighed. "There aren't a lot of girls my age around here, and even if Eastlake is a decent school, I don't hang out much there. I'm a little rusty at making friends myself, but hey, you had a book. It seemed like a sign or something."

"True enough," Bella said. Her grip on *A Christmas Carol* loosened.

The wind blew the last of the brown leaves off a nearby tree, and Layney caught one. She twirled it by the stem. "I thought maybe we could eventually be friends or at least hang out together." Layney glanced up, and a grin appeared. "Besides, holiday break can be super boring. I avoid the apartment as much as I can, or my aunt will put me to work."

"What kind of work?" The warm winter sun disappeared behind clouds and Bella shivered. "Does your aunt have an online store or something?"

"If only!" Layney grimaced. "A few years back, I made the mistake of telling my aunt I was bored, and she told me to clean the fridge and the closets."

"Ew!" Bella's nose wrinkled at the thought of cleaning, but a very unwelcome suspicion reared its ugly head. Would she have to learn to clean a fridge? Or worse, a *toilet*?"

Layney continued, "Anyhoo, since I don't have school work to do, and I don't want my aunt to put me to work, I was glad to see you."

"You were watching me?" Bella shot a nervous look over her shoulder.

"I saw you out my front room window. And no, I'm not really spying. It faces the pool like it does in all the apartments." Layney smiled tentatively. "I only had to look to know the new girl was here."

Bella relaxed a little. "Fair enough." She sighed. "The thing is I'm used to a lot of alone time. I had a large room and library in my old house. I read for hours, and no one bothered me." Bella grasped her book tighter.

Layney winced. "I'm sorry I disturbed your solitude, but..." She raised her brows. "I know! We could go to the public library. It's not that far from here."

Bella scrunched her nose. "I've never been to a public library. The one in my former home had everything I needed or wanted." She covered her mouth. "I sounded too snooty, didn't I?"

"I'll ignore it. You haven't been poor long enough to talk like one of us." Layney teased. "But seriously, do you want to go to the library? There's a place we can sit and read. Then you won't be disturbed, but it gets me out of any chores my aunt might think of me to do." Bella thought about it. "Is it close enough to walk?"

"You said you have a bicycle?" Layney asked.

Bella nodded.

Layney grinned widely. "Go get it and meet me here. We can easily ride our bikes to the library."

When Bella wheeled her candy-apple red bike to the tarped pool, Layney waited with her purple rusted one. Bella's bike sparkled like brand new compared to Layney's—she no longer thought it lame.

Both girls wisely donned their winter coats, boots, and gloves, but Bella felt overdressed next to Layney's worn jacket. She adjusted her trendy backpack over her shoulder and reminded herself that her new friend hadn't seemed to mind the difference.

Layney flashed Bella a warm smile. "Nice ride!"

"Thanks." Bella bit back a comment about how it was one of the few things her parents hadn't bought with credit."

"The library isn't far from here with two wheels, but it takes a little too long to get there if you have to walk." Layney hopped onto her white seat and motioned to Bella. "Follow me."

Bella followed suit, though her mind was scarcely on the trip itself. Instead, she mentally contrasted Layney with her old friends, who had laughed at her "juvenile" present of a bicycle and shamed her out of riding it. Layney, though, rode through the increasing cold, pointing out local landmarks, warning her of potholes, and saying things like, "*The Dollar Store* sells the best generic macaroni and cheese. Four boxes for only a..."

When they finally reached the public library Bella was impressed by the classy tan-bricked building. As they entered through the automated doors, her eyes widened in surprise over the decorative nooks and crannies that surrounded the shelves of books. It was nothing like the old libraries seen on movies or television. The children's section had a huge fake tree in the middle of a green carpet made to look like grass. On the branches were fairies and colorful fantasy woodland creatures. Bella was already mesmerized by the place.

Layney whispered, "Let's go over in that section to read." She pointed to a corner with soft brown leather chairs and quaint little tables.

Both girls plopped down into the seats and pulled out their own books they had brought to read. They spoke softly about the stories and then got lost among the words.

They had such a good time that day that they repeated their trek to the library three days in a row, and Bella became more comfortable around Layney. They mostly discussed books, but sometimes Layney shared details about Eastlake High and the boys in their complex who attended there.

On the third trip home from the library, Layney complained, "There are some things I don't like about public libraries." She pedaled slowly because they had to dodge a few pedestrians. "One, we can't talk at a normal volume and two, we can't snack. Whenever I read, I get snacky. Also, I wish I owned the books to read whenever I want."

Bella rode next to her once the path widened and was free from people. "I sometimes want to eat a treat, but it really doesn't bother me too much." She emitted a quiet sigh. "I wish we could keep the books also." All of Bella's favorites wouldn't fit in their apartment and she had to leave behind too many.

"Let's take a different route." Layney gestured to turn left. "I want to show you this creepy, but cool looking house."

Bella asked, "I need to get home before dark. Is it close?"

"It will only take a few extra minutes from our normal trip." Layney pedaled a little faster and Bella kept up with her speed.

They ended up in the outskirts of town, but Gastonville was small, and true to her word, the house wasn't that much out of their way. They rode past a few scattered homes with mailboxes, then Layney led Bella to a long, bricked driveway enclosed behind an ornate iron gate and fence. The lavish boundary encircled a yard overgrown with brown grass and shriveled flowers. Even in winter's dormancy, the out-of-control garden was clearly dead. Bella knew neglect when she saw it. Her old home had never been so shabby.

But what made Bella's jaw drop was the abandoned red-brick Victorian home that loomed over the decrepit yard. Peeling white gingerbread trim and faded burgundy gables stood tall against the gray winter sky. Several cracked or missing windows brought horror movies to mind.

"What do you think?" Layney asked while she got off her bike.

Bella scrunched her face. "It looks haunted."

"I think it's beautiful despite its eerie vibe." Layney's expression softened. "I pretend it's a magical castle up on some European mountain top." She moved off her seat and put the kickstand in place.

Bella tilted her head. For someone like Layney, the turret and decorative trim on the house might have a fairy-tale feel, but Bella had visited European castles. Comparing this house to a fortress was a stretch of the imagination.

Still, she said, "I guess if you ignore most of the disrepair, it does kind of look like a castle."

Layney motioned, "Come on, let's go inside." She stood directly in front of the iron gate.

"We'll be late getting home." Bella had gotten off her bike and was standing while holding the handlebars.

Layney turned to face Bella. "I have a confession to make." Her lips turned up mischievously. "I've been inside many times. It has a library that's better than the public one and it's literally too magical to describe. You'll have to see to believe it, because my attempts to explain it would be impossible."

Bella put her kickstand down. "Why didn't you tell me about this place before?"

"I would have the first day we met after I discovered you liked books, but we didn't really know each other." Layney stood in front of Bella. "Think about it. A strange girl wants to take you to an abandoned house and you're supposed to trust her?"

"You have a good point." Bella agreed.

"We left the library earlier today, but I understand you want to get home." Layney looked back at the house. "What about we go inside tomorrow? Are you up for some adventure?"

Bella was curious about how the house looked inside, but wasn't that trespassing? "Who owns this place? I don't want to get into trouble."

"I heard the old lady that lived there didn't have any family and no will to deed it to." Layney got back onto her bike. "It's small-town gossip, but either way, I've been using the library inside for years and haven't ever been disturbed."

Bella hoisted herself onto the bike's seat and the girls pedaled back home. They were unusually quiet; their normal chatter was absent. They typically discussed what they had read or checked out from the library. Bella's mind whirled over the concept of more shelves to explore, but it still seemed forbidden despite what Layney had said about it.

When they reached Castle Creek, Layney suggested, "Meet me at our same time and place tomorrow?"

Bella nodded.

Layney added, "We'll go to my magical oasis." Then she winked.

Bella said tentatively, "Okay."

She wanted a library like the one she left behind in her old home. She wanted to have friends she could enjoy doing things with to replace all the things she had to give up. That didn't mean she was gullible enough to believe the abandoned house contained a library full of fantastical things. She would go tomorrow and see for herself what Layney thinks is a "magical oasis".

Chapter 2

Bellarose

A thin layer of white covered the drab parts of the Castle Creek atrium. The crisp smell of snow lingered in the cool air. It was a typical Colorado winter where one day the sun warmed you into a false sense that you could leave your coat behind only to turn into a blizzard on the same day. Thankfully, there wasn't any wind or blustering snow. It was more of a pure Christmas powder where *all is calm and all is bright*.

Layney was waiting in the designated meeting place with her rusted bicycle. Bella walked the red bike up to her. The contrast between the girl's belongings wasn't as obvious to Bella once she looked past material items and more at the girl she was beginning to view as a friend.

Bella had a thicker puffy red coat for the cooler temperatures, but Layney still wore her thinner worn army surplus jacket.

She knew Layney better, but did she dare—? "Do you want to borrow one of my thicker coats? It's colder today."

Layney shook her head. "No, I'm fine. This is warmer than it looks." She zipped it up and stuck on a black stocking cap that contrasted with her blonde hair.

They both put on gloves and were wearing boots, which made pedaling a bicycle a little more difficult but they were prepared for the journey.

"We may need to move slower if the paths haven't been cleared of snow." Layney's breath showed in the cold air.

Bella agreed. "It could be worse if they cleared the paths. At least snow gives a little more traction than ice. I've taken a spill on my bike in the driveway of my old house. The groundskeeper had cleared the snow, but, well, that doesn't matter." Bella blew out air and saw it float above her head. "We have time to go slower."

When they reached the Victorian home, Bella observed, "The sparkling snow takes away a little of its horror movie vibe, but not completely."

"You're funny." Layney chuckled as she opened the gate and they walked their bikes up to the stairs that led to the front door.

"I think it looks like a death trap." Bella put her kickstand down and scanned the house. "Am I going to fall through any of the floorboards?"

Layney laughed. "You're being paranoid. It's totally safe. The floors are solid. I've been on them plenty of times." She used the stairs and motioned for Bella to follow. "The place is only neglected on the outside. Inside is another story."

Layney turned the knob and the door creaked open—a perfect sound for a scary movie. Bella half-expected to see a psycho who kept his dead mom's body in the living room or maybe, since it was around the holidays, a visit from the ghost of Christmas future.

Bella whispered, "You're sure we're not trespassing?"

"I'm positive." Layney grinned but continued inside.

Bella shut the door behind her and quickly the qualms were forgotten by the extraordinary sight. No dusty cobwebs hung from the sparkling crystal chandelier. The high-vaulted foyer ceiling and white marble floors reminded Bella of her former home.

"Wow!" Bella gasped. "This is not what I expected at all!"

"I told you! It's magical! This isn't even the best part. Follow me." Layney led her down a hallway, past a formal dining room and parlor to large double doors with engravings of books carved into the wood. She shoved open the right-hand door and stepped aside.

Inside was an immense room full of tall shelves overflowing with books. Even Bella's posh home didn't have a library like this. A spiral staircase at the end of the room led to a second floor of bookshelves that encircled the library.

An aura of something other-worldly permeated the room.

"How..." Bella stepped inside. "This is massive! How does it even fit inside the house?"

Layney just grinned.

A crackle drew Bella's attention to the welcoming fireplace in the center of the library. Stunned, she took off her coat and draped it over the cozy furniture facing the fire. The chairs looked like the ones her mother had picked out for her father's office. They were plush but perfect for hunkering down to read a good book.

Embossed signs indicated literary genres, and on the other side of the room, a ladder stood propped against the shelves.

"No way." She ran over to the ladder, climbed up and down, then pushed it. "It has wheels! It's like the library in *Beauty and the Beast*."

"Exactly," Layney crossed her arms. "But look up."

When Bella craned her neck to the high domed ceiling, however, she let out a muted scream. "Is that—did I see a mermaid jump out of that ceiling?" She stared open-mouthed at the murals of fantastical creatures, then laughed. "No way! The mermaid left, and a unicorn replaced her?"

"Yes!" Layney sighed happily. "It's like the great Leonardo da Vinci himself painted those creatures except they're magical."

Both girls giggled, their eyes still on the creatures frolicking in and out of the painted ceiling.

Bella turned to Layney. "What is this place?"

"It's my secret. Well, now it's our secret." Layney smiled. "This place is literally magical."

Bella knitted her brows. "Yes, but how does a place like this even exist?"

"I don't know." Layney grabbed Bella's hand and led her to the chairs for them to sit. "When I first arrived here, it looked like a typical abandoned house with dust and cobwebs, but I began to wish for things and they appeared." Layney waved her hand like a wand. "The books and shelves were always here, but not all this other stuff like the ladder."

"I don't understand what you mean." Bella was confused.

"It's easier to show you."

Layney walked to the ladder and scooted it down to the middle section of the shelves. She climbed up a few steps and passed her hand over some spines until she pulled out a red one. She descended the ladder and walked back to hand it to Bella.

"*Christmas Home Interior Decorating?*" Bella frowned. "I don't see your point."

"Look through that book." Layney tapped it. "Find something you think would look good in this room."

Still confused, Bella played along. She turned the pages until she found a photo of trimmings that would look perfect.

"Here." She handed the book back to Layney. "These would look good."

Suddenly the room began to fill with evergreen garlands wrapped in gold, silver, and red ribbons. The sweet scents of cinnamon, spices, and pine wafted through the room. A tall fir tree popped out of mid-air, as she watched garlands, lights, and ornaments fly onto the tree, making it match the ones in the book.

Bella rubbed her eyes. "What is going on here?" She swallowed hard. "This is impossible!"

Layney's voice pitched higher, "Like I said before, you had to see to believe. That's not all." Her face brightened. "Are you hungry?"

"I'm not too—"

"Wouldn't a nice cup of hot chocolate filled with marshmallows and a plate of Christmas cookies hit the spot?"

"Well, yes, but—"

Two piping-hot cups of cocoa and a plate of frosted, holiday shaped treats appeared on the table in between Bella and Layney's lounge chairs.

"What?" Bella stared wide-eyed. "How are you doing that?"

"I'm not," Layney replied. "Now let's have two Christmas stockings hang from the mantelpiece with cats wearing Santa hats embroidered onto them."

Bella thought she heard a popping sound like a genie coming out from his bottle as two stockings suddenly appeared on the fireplace shelf.

She gasped and rubbed her eyes. "No way! How are you doing that?"

Layney gave a mischievous grin. "This house—or the books—are making it happen. I don't know where the magic is coming from. I only know anything in those books can become real."

"What happens if I read a book about dragons? Do they suddenly appear?"

Layney shook her head. "No, fictional books are a different magic than the non-fiction. The Christmas decoration book was non-fiction.

Bella inspected a cookie. "This wasn't in that book you handed to me."

"That's the great thing, if what I want is in one of those books,"—Layney pointed to the non-fiction section"—I say I want it, and it will appear. The treats I conjured up were inside a cookbook I found in this library, and the stockings were in a book about things you can make for cats."

Bella put the cookie down. "You're saying fiction books are different? What happens with a novel?" When Layney delayed answering by taking a sip of cocoa, Bella asked, "Do you only read nonfiction? Have you read fiction in here?"

"Of course!" Layney beamed. "That's the best part of this library, because you get to experience adventure like none you've never had before."

Bella scooted to the edge of her seat. "How?"

Layney sipped her cocoa before answering. "It's scary but exciting. I read a book about an evil fairy who changed a prince into a dragon. His soon-to-be fiancé found out and tried to save him." Layney's brows knitted. "I... I became the fiancé in the story and got turned into a dragon, but I turned back to myself at the end."

Bella arched an eyebrow. "Okay, yes, I see there are magic cookies and a Christmas tree, but..." A chill ran down Bella's back. "You can't honestly be telling me you become part of a book?"

"Yes." Layney nodded. "And no time passes in the real world. You can read a whole book in one sitting, become one of the characters, and return here seconds later at the end of the story."

Bella's mind spun. She absentmindedly picked a Christmas tree-shaped cookie and took a bite, washing it down with the cocoa while processing the information. Yes, she'd seen the decorations and the food appear, but this was ridiculous.

"Okay, I'm beginning to think this is all some elaborate hoax." Bella set down her mug and crossed her arms. "It has to be. And, I find it hard to believe you can read a book without time passing. But the hardest part to accept is that you become one of the characters in the story."

"As I said before, seeing is believing."

"But what if you become a villain? Do you get to choose which character you are?"

"You'll have to read one of those books and find out for yourself. But not today." Layney looked at her phone, stood, and started putting on the jacket she had discarded. "Though time doesn't pass when you're reading, a lot of time has passed since we got here. We need to go before my dad gets home from work."

"Wait!" Bella touched Layney's arm. "You show me this fantastical place, and we already have to leave?"

"Yes, but we can come back." Layney handed Bella her coat.

"When?"

"Probably tomorrow." A worried look crossed her face. "But promise me you won't tell anyone about this."

"I definitely won't." Bella put on her coat, then pulled the long brown hair trapped inside under her collar. "No one would believe me anyway."

"True, but also, well…" Layney pulled a necklace with a teardrop pendant from underneath the scarf at her neck. "When I first found this place and realized what it could do, I started looking for ways to protect this house's secrets. I found a book of spells, and then this appeared around my neck. I think it gives me magical abilities when I'm inside here."

Bella examined the dangling pendant, then narrowed her eyes at her new friend. "It doesn't look magical, and you said you weren't making this happen."

"It is, and I'm not." She drew a deep breath. "The library is, but I couldn't have anyone find out what is going on here. That's when I remembered something about vampires not being able to enter homes if they weren't invited. I wished for that, and when I left that afternoon, people who passed me, didn't notice the house at all. It doesn't even get junk mail anymore."

"I saw it."

"Yes, but I brought you here. You can see the house, but no one else can."

Bella pressed her lips together. The amazing room transformations and treats appearing from thin-air had to be a trick of her mind. Magic didn't exist in the world—or did it? Would these books transport her into the stories? She had no way of testing Layney's claim to have a spell that prevented trespassing. Bella pulled on her gloves. For now, she'd return, if only to make sure she hadn't dreamed the whole thing.

The girls rode their bikes back to the apartments in silence. The trip seemed faster, and Bella's mind dashed over the past hours.

As they walked their bikes beyond the tarped pool, Layney asked, "You want to meet tomorrow afternoon? We can go back."

Bella nodded. "Sure. After all, I want to read one of your books." She chuckled. "I'll probably be dreaming about magical libraries tonight."

"Cool. I'll see you tomorrow, then." With a wave, Layney climbed the outside steps.

Bella watched her go, then locked her bike to the rack in front of her apartment and let herself in.

The lonely, unfamiliar smell of the apartment had nothing in common with Layney's secret library. Magic or not, she had to return tomorrow to see for herself. Losing herself in a book didn't sound so awful, no matter what Layney said.

Chapter 3

Bellarose

After a sleepless night, Bella showered for rejuvenation. It was horrible sharing the space with her parents, because she had to carry a tote with her own toiletries rather than store them under the sink. The low powered water from the shower head still managed to wake her up, but she was thankful for winter break. Normally insomniac nights meant applying extra concealer for the bags under her eyes, but the more affordable generic makeup wasn't going to do the trick.

Bella's conflicting emotions bounced between guilt for not helping her parents, who were miserable, and excitement about returning to the magnificent library and its shelves of books. Poor Mom. She'd always been at home for Bella, but now she was stuck in a temporary job at the department store. And Dad? She could almost see him like he was at dinner, slouched over his chicken-rice casserole.

"My job is horrible, but it pays the bills," he'd mumbled. "I need to look for something better after Christmas."

Thinking about her parents' slumped shoulders made her own sag, but she wanted to channel Layney's gumption. Her friend had faced life without a mom. Her life wasn't at its worst, and perhaps instead of crying over things she couldn't control, she needed to figure out what she could manage.

Practical determination won over the anticipation of returning to Layney's secret library. She'd help out. With an exaggerated yawn, Bella gathered the laundry. She'd never done it before, but how hard could it be? Besides, Castle Creek's laundry facility wasn't far from her apartment, and Mom had set aside money specifically for the job on the counter.

Confident that she could easily manage the task, she held the basket of dirty clothes on her hip while shoving the coins into her pocket. Once she left the apartment, though, Layney's words from the day before echoed in her memory. Everyone had a window view to the pool area, which she had to pass on her way to the laundry room. Every window seemed to hide people, and she felt eyes watching her every step.

She'd never imagined entering a laundry facility would provide relief, but her shoulders relaxed when she closed the door. A warm clean-linen scent enveloped the room. There were only two washers, and one was filled with wet clothes. She dumped her basket in the empty machine, then stopped. The detergent! How had she forgotten detergent! A vending machine in the corner offered small boxes of powder soap, but she only had enough money for one load to wash and dry.

It was only a short trip back to the apartment but could she leave the clothes? No, it wasn't worth the risk of someone stealing them. Cursing, Bella pulled out the dirty clothes, put them in the basket, and lugged it to the apartment. Again, she felt the watchful eyes of apartment dwellers even if she couldn't see them. Holding the basket and unlocking the door was harder than she'd thought it'd be, but she managed. She set the basket and the keys on the table and turned to look for the detergent. The search wasn't long, and she cursed again. There it was. Right next to the coin jar. Why hadn't she noticed it?

She tossed the blue bottle into the basket, heaved out a huge sigh, and backed out of her apartment.

The sound of water filling the machine greeted her when she again entered the clean smelling room. Clothes sloshed around and around behind the door's glass window and the other machine was still occupied.

"Ugh! Now what do I do?"

Still unsure about leaving her clothes behind. Bella hefted the basket and trudged back to her apartment. As she reached her apartment door, though, realization smacked her. She'd left the keys on the kitchen table.

"Worst Christmas break ever."

Tears welled up, but before they fell, she remembered Mr. Fitz. The superintendent of the building probably had a master key to let her into the apartment. She balanced the heavy basket of soap and dirty clothes on her hip and walked down to Mr. Fitz's and knocked on the door.

"I'm coming. I'm coming."

After a moment, a gray-haired man opened the door. He tugged his worn-out gray cardigan sweater closer over his plaid shirt. "Yes?"

She set down her basket. "Hi, Mr. Fitz. I'm Bellarose Bonnay from apartment 6A."

"Ah, yes. Your family moved in not so long ago. I may be older than dirt, but my mind is as sharp as a tack." Mr. Fitz laughed heartily, and Bella instantly liked him.

"The thing is," she said in a rush, "I managed to lock myself out. I wanted to do laundry but the washer is being used."

He glanced down at the basket of clothes. "It's tricky learning to share a washing machine with a bunch of strangers, but soon you'll get used to it." He smiled. "Also, you'll learn to trust the people. You could've left that basket next to the machines. I imagine it's burdensome carrying it back and forth."

"It's not too bad," Bella lied.

He chuckled, then he gave her a sheepish grin. "I confess I saw you go to the laundry room with a basket of clothes and no soap. When you returned to your apartment after only a minute, I figured you realized your mistake." He put his hands in his pockets. "My advice is, unless you like hanging out for an hour or so while your clothes get washed, it's easier to leave them behind."

She exhaled. "Did you guess about my keys, too?"

"Follow me." He stepped outside his door. "I'll get you back inside your apartment as fast as my old legs will take me."

Mr. Fitz hobbled, jingling like Santa's sleigh with his utility belt full of keys. She hefted the basket into her arms again—and admitted to herself that he was right about its weight.

He unlocked and opened the apartment door. "There you go, Miss Bonnay."

"Thank you, Mr. Fitz."

"You're welcome," he said. "Have a good day."

Bella plopped the basket on the small dining table. After her failed attempt at something as simple as laundry, everything seemed worse. Her determination was beginning to wane. The whole area, which was tinier than Bella's old bedroom, seemed to shrink. The late morning light made the thrift store avocado sofa even shabbier. The sunken-in cushions were cringe-worthy. She didn't want to be here. She really wanted to meet Layney at the pool, but something whispered that she should help her parents too.

She decided to prepare dinner. The cupboards were sparse, but the bright orange and blue box of macaroni and cheese stood out to her. Mac and cheese shouldn't be hard. Anyone could make it. She didn't care that she had similar thoughts about the laundry. She checked the clock. If she started it now, she'd be able to meet Layney, and her parents could reheat it for dinner. Bella grinned. Pasta with powdered cheese? Not a problem.

A half an hour later, however, the smoke alarm blared, and the acrid smell of burnt cheese and noodles filled the small space. Bella put down *A Christmas Carol* and rushed to turn off the burner. Then she switched on the stove fan. She threw open the windows, but when she pulled the front door open, Layney was standing, her hand raised to knock.

"Hey girl, what's going on?" Layney sniffed the air. "Are you okay? What happened?"

Bella fanned the door open and close to air out the apartment.

"I was trying to make dinner so my mom wouldn't have to cook when she got home from work tonight."

"It's almost noon." Layney's left brow rose. "Why are you starting so early?"

Bella stepped aside to let Layney in. "I wanted to go with you to the magical library, but I wanted to help my parents out first. I didn't know if I would make it home in time."

"Oh, Bella," Layney said. For a moment, Bella thought the other girl might hug her, but she only patted her shoulder. "Magic, remember? Time is weird there. Even with the trip up and back we've got time." Layney's nose scrunched as she stepped into the apartment and headed for the kitchen. "What were you trying to make, anyway?"

Bella lifted the scorched sauce-pan. "Macaroni and cheese."

"That doesn't reheat too great. It would have been dry to eat. Tell you what! I promise to help you prepare dinner after we go to the castle today. I'm a decent cook. My aunt has chili in the crockpot, and I helped her make it." Layney looked over at the laundry Bella left out.

She bit her lower lip. "I'll help you with your laundry too. I saw you walking back and forth with your clothes."

Bella palmed her face. "I'm not keen on the idea of living in a fishbowl."

"Sorry, Although, there are perks."

"I can't think of any."

"When you're bored, you can spy on the other tenants too." Layney's smile stretched in a Cheshire cat grin. "Maybe you'll get a peek at Gerard. He's so fetch."

Bella tilted her head. "Fetch?"

"I heard that on a movie that had a bunch of stuck-up rich girls. He's fetching. You know, attractive."

"Yeah." Bella's ego prickled at the rich girl reference. "I've seen the movie. It's outdated."

Layney continued, apparently oblivious to Bella's discomfort. "Well, Gerard is hot, but he knows it. The only time his pride got put down a few notches was last summer."

"What happened?"

"He put too much soap into the washing machine." Layney chuckled. "The soap bubbles filled the laundry room and flowed into the pool. I laughed so hard I thought I would pee my pants. We were swimming with bubbles all summer."

Bella grinned. It sounded more like a TV sitcom than real life. But that brought her laundry episode to mind, and she frowned.

"I'm glad it was him and not me. I've never done laundry before and I may have repeated his mistake." She scraped the inedible pasta into the trash. "Burning dinner was bad enough. With all the nosy neighbors around, I would've become the new joke."

Layney shook her head. "No, don't worry. I'll teach you how to do laundry too. There's kind of an unwritten schedule around here. We'll figure out when your family should use the facility. It'll be okay."

Bella put the sauce pan in the sink with water to soak.

"I meant that offer. We can go to my castle now, and then I'll help you clean up and make dinner when we get back."

Bella eyed the kitchen, paused, and then faced Layney. "Okay, I'll let you help me cook tonight."

Bella grabbed her coat and followed the smiling Layney, but before the door closed, Bella checked her pocket for the key. She'd learned that lesson already.

Layney had brought her bike to Bella's apartment. Bella had her bicycle locked to a rack nearby. As they walked their bikes past the courtyard, Bella snuck a peek at the other apartments. It really was like a hotel atrium. Every apartment had one door and lone large window facing the center.

When they reached the pool area, a guy with wavy black hair strode toward them. Maybe strutted was a better word. Bella tried not to stare. She couldn't quite determine his age, but he had broad shoulders and may have been about six feet tall.

Layney whispered. "Speak of the devil, that's Gerard." She huffed. "Don't look too hard, or he may think you're in love with him."

"He's huge," Bella said softly. "How old is he?"

"He's our age." Layney continued walking. "I could introduce you."

"No thanks. He's not my type."

Layney grinned. "He's definitely my type, but he's too full of himself." They neared the exit gate. "Anyway, let's go to the castle. I want to show you how the books work."

Doubt snuck back in. It couldn't possibly be as wonderful as it had seemed yesterday, could it? Bella hesitated, then said, "I'm not sure I totally believe in magic, but I couldn't sleep last night thinking about it. Despite my former life, I haven't experienced everything extraordinary."

"You mean money can't buy everything?" Layney said tartly.

"No," Bella snapped and then frowned. "Well, it definitely can't transport people into the stories. I'm still struggling to accept that concept."

Layney's response was a wide grin. "Seeing is believing."

Bella had seen many wonders of the world, but even after visiting the pyramids in Egypt, she realized that man-made ingenuity can seem supernatural when it isn't. She hoped the library delivered on convincing her as Layney claimed it would, because that would mean she was about to plunge into a fantastical story.

Chapter 4

Bellarose

G erard blocked their way to the exit and planted himself in front of Layney and Bella's bikes. His stunt interrupted Bella's thoughts of the possibility of physically experiencing a fairy tale.

She looked up at him and he winked. She rolled her eyes in response and Layney smirked.

Gerard asked, "Layney, who's your friend?"

"Don't play dumb." Layney looked at Bella. "You know she's the new tenant from 6A."

"I know, but what's her name?"

His cocky grin made Bella cringe. She knew his type from her former school. "*She* can speak for herself. My name is Bellarose, but most people call me Bella."

Layney added, "Bella is French for beautiful."

Gerard looked her up and down. "It suits her."

"Layney, we need to go." Bella hopped onto her bicycle. "Move, please."

Gerard refused to budge. "Don't you want to know my name?"

"Nope."

Her answer didn't faze him. He waggled his eyebrows. "Probably because you already know it."

"Yep."

Bella rode her bicycle around him, but a shorter, brown-haired boy with his nose in a book walked in front of her bike. She squeezed the hand brakes and skidded to a stop.

The boy fumbled and looked up. "Oh! Sorry, I didn't see you."

Though her heart was pounding at the near accident, she managed a smile. "*A Christmas Carol* is the best. I read it every December."

"Hey, book nerd," Gerard mocked. "You should watch where you're going or you'll end up walking into a busy street.

The boy blushed, but Layney chimed in before Gerard could say anything else. "Bella, this is Quinn. He lives in 3D and goes to our school too."

"Nice to meet you, Quinn," Bella said with a smile before giving Gerard a dirty look.

Quinn cleared his throat. "Uh, yes, nice to meet you too. Maybe we can talk sometime about this book? I mean, that's if you're into talking about—"

"Dude, you're such a nerd!" Gerard cut in. "Girls have better things to do than talk about books."

Bella scowled at Gerard. "And what would those be?"

"Don't you all like to discuss hair and makeup?" He straightened. "Also, you probably go on about how dashingly handsome the young men who live here are. Layney could give you the inside scoop on all of that, FYI," he added, and his eyebrows rose, "I'm single."

"Girls are not all vapid creatures who pine over egotistical boys." Bella clenched her handlebars. "If you had any intelligence, you would put more time into reading than flirting with a girl who isn't interested in you!"

Quinn gave her a crooked smile, but Gerard glared.

Layney flinched.

Bella frowned. It wasn't the best first impression. Still, she squared her shoulders. Too bad she didn't care. She'd never been able to stand either bullies or boys who thought too highly of themselves. It didn't matter that Gerard was cute. She didn't like how he talked down to her or to Quinn.

"All things considered," Layney interrupted. "I think we better be on our way if we're going to get back before supper."

They rode away, but Bella glanced back to see if the boys were watching them. They were.

Once out of earshot, Layney said, "You shouldn't have been so mean to Gerard. He really isn't a jerk. He can be a good guy, but when a nice, shiny, new girl comes to the apartments, he over compensates."

"Being rude isn't overcompensating." Bella glanced at Layney, then swerved around a pothole. "I know you think he's fetch or gorgeous or whatever, but he shouldn't have been mean to Quinn."

"No," Layney agreed. "He shouldn't have. Perhaps he needed to be taken down a notch, but maybe not that way."

Bella snorted. "With his ego, I'm sure he'll get over it. I'm also certain he has girls who will fill his head with visions of grandeur without help from either of us."

They rode for a few minutes before she added, "And thinking that girls only talk about makeup? I like talking about books more than hair and makeup." She shot a side-look at Layney. "*This* former rich girl wasn't a shallow mean girl like the movies portray."

"Sorry. I guess I deserve that." Layney sighed.

A little out-of-breath, the girls reached the house, though getting there seemed to take less time now that Bella knew the way. For a brief moment the house looked blurry, like a mirage off in a distant desert oasis. The closer they got to the building, however, the more in focus it became. Were her eyes playing tricks on her? Perhaps Layney did put some kind of spell on the place to keep it hidden.

"I wish Gerard was ugly," Layney said out of the blue as she pulled out the golden pendant. "I like to think I'm fairly sensible, but when he's around..." She grimaced. "What did you say a few minutes ago? Vapid. I feel vapid and superficial around Gerard."

"You aren't, though," Bella assured her. Then, she laughed. "Don't worry. I'm sure we can find a nice, juicy story about a duke or Scotland laird to get your mind off Gerard."

They walked their bikes through the iron gate and put the kickstands down once they reached the front steps. They moved up the stairs and through the stained-glass doors. Yesterday, Bella hadn't noticed the beautiful designs. She'd been too worried about seeing a specter. Today, she noticed the glass doors' depictions of famous fairy tales but she didn't linger to examine the patterns, because she was too eager to dive into a new book. Even if they didn't actually transport her as Layney claimed, reading was an adventure. The magical library was a book worm's candy store—filled to the brim with delicious books.

Bella and Layney rushed through the beautiful halls, and when they entered the room, all the decorations Bella had wished from the holiday decor book remained. She closed her eyes and breathed in the pine, cinnamon, and wood burning scents that erased the stress of laundry, charred pasta and Gerard's egotistical comments. She hadn't hallucinated yesterday.

"Was that fire going all night?" Bella asked.

"No, I only thought of it as we entered the house to warm up this room."

The girls peeled off their jackets and set them over an expensive chair.

This year, the holidays had been hard, but here, with her new friend, in this festive library, she felt at home.

She eyed the table that had held the cookies and hot chocolate the day before. "Where are the treats? We didn't finish them yesterday."

"No, snacks don't stay like the decorations. I tested it once. I left the room for a few minutes, and when I returned, the food was gone." Layney brushed her hand over the table where the treats were. "If it stayed, it would spoil or attract mice or something. I can't come here every day."

Bella shuddered and looked at the floor for rodents. "Why can't you?"

"School, homework, and chores. You know, the normal stuff."

Bella hadn't experienced chores until recently, but she understood what Layney meant when she mentioned school and homework. That's what had kept her from regular reading for fun and was why she loved the Christmas break.

Bella couldn't stop looking at the books. "What should I read first? Hmm…" She skimmed the signs labeled Fantasy. "I know! What about that book where you became a dragon?"

Layney eyed her skeptically.

"What? I want to experience becoming a dragon."

"It was scary. Are you sure?"

Bella nodded. "You said that once the story ends, I'll return back to being me. I don't see why not."

Layney called out, "Bring me *The Scorned Fae*."

A red-covered book flew off the shelf and into Layney's hand.

Bella's eyes widened. "What?"

"If I know the title of the book, I can ask for it by name. The library will give it to me." Layney handed it to Bella. "I told you this place is magical."

"*The Scorned Fae* is an intriguing title." Bella flipped through the pages. "I think I will like this, but it isn't very long."

"It's a short story. You'll finish it quickly. Maybe when you complete it, you'll want to read another one." Layney pulled the ladder over to the fantasy section Bella was browsing. "I was planning on reading something longer." She climbed the rolling ladder. "I think the clock will stop for both of us if we're reading at the same time. Since you're the first person to be here with me, I've never tested it."

Bella tilted her head up toward Layney. "What are you going to choose?"

"I was looking for a fairy tale or something similar. I don't know." Layney scooted the ladder along the shelves, pulled out books, inspected the covers, and put them back. Finally, she selected a purple volume from the top shelf.

"How do you even know where to begin to look?"

"I've had a lot of time to peruse the shelves. I don't know every title, but I know many. That shelf is mostly fairy tales"—Layney gestured to the books—"but they aren't the familiar tales I grew up with. The stories change and twist in unexpected ways."

"That sounds even better than a prince turning into a dragon."

"While I'm still on the ladder, do you want me to find you a lengthier book?"

"Yes. I can read *The Scorned Fae* another time."

Bella slid the short story inside her jeans' back pocket. It would be a good bed-time story.

Without any hesitation, Layney grabbed a blue tome and then descended. She handed the story to Bella, and they moved to the lounge chairs in front of the crackling fireplace.

Layney eyed the empty table. "Are you hungry? Do you want anything to snack on while you read?"

"I thought I became a character in the story. How can I eat if I'm not here?"

"Well, you can stop any time you want, graze a little and start back where you left off." Layney rubbed her hand over her book. "It's a little like being in a play, except the costumes and sets are real. All you have to do is mentally concentrate on your desire to leave the story, and you're back here in reality."

Even if Layney was exaggerating, just being in this library was an escape. Bella was going to play along. She didn't want to go back to her dreary apartment.

"Okay then, I'll have a peppermint mocha latte and sugar cook—" The latte and cookies started to materialize but faded when she added, "Wait! I'd rather have gingerbread cookies."

A plate of smiling gingerbread men appeared next to a steaming mug with a candy cane hanging over the edge and a snowman-shaped mug topped with whipped cream. The cookies smelled freshly baked, and the minty coffee scent was better than anything Bella had before.

"My mom and I used to make these treats every Christmas." She picked one up. Her eyes watered. "That's not going to happen this year."

Layney didn't say anything, only took a sip.

Bella bit a small portion of the cookie. It melted into her mouth. She tried the drink, and the liquid warmed her throat. "That is the best latte I've ever had. It isn't too hot either—the perfect temperature."

"I know exactly what you mean." Layney wiped off her whipped cream mustache. "When I think of Christmas magic, this place always comes to mind." She chomped on the gingerbread man. "In the summer, I drink cold things like iced tea or soda. This time of year is more magical."

Christmas is like that for me, too." Bella finished her cookie and swallowed more of the latte. She raised her book like she was offering a toast. "Right then. We read!"

Chapter 5

Bellarose

B ella settled back into the chair and moaned in happy anticipation. Whether or not Layney was right about the story's world becoming real, it was nice to be comfortable and have a new book. Without another glance at her new friend, Bella dove into the pages.

Prologue: Aerowyn

Timeless tales of beauties and beasts would have not been written without someone like Aerowyn the enchantress.

Exquisite and ever-changing beauty like Aerowyn's couldn't be captured in a painting. Golden hair that sparkled as diamond dust would transform into rich chestnut brown hair and then to raven locks in the blink of an eye. Humans never saw her true visage that was ever-changing.

Her eyes, too, altered with her moods. Ice blue meant she was feeling apathy, while chocolate brown reflected her warmth and graciousness. Her eyes flashed violet when they revealed her unpredictable nature, and this was when she was the most dangerous.

The enchantress's ability to morph into many different people made her more frightening than any other being in all the land. No one knew who she really was, but no matter her disguise, the one constant was the gold chain with a tear-drop shaped pendant she wore around her neck.

Though terrifying, her powers were meant to do good. Her true goal was to change unkindness and selfishness into redemption and generos-

ity, but those who neglected the less fortunate and refused to change their ways faced condemnation.

Without Aerowyn, this story would have never been told.

Bella paused, used her fingers to mark the spot, and glanced around the library. She still sat in a completely normal, enchanted library, but that a magic library was normal nearly made her laugh. A quick glance at the other chair had her covering her mouth with her hand to keep quiet. Layney seemed transfixed by her book. Nothing was quite as irritating as having a good story interrupted. Instead of commenting, Bella drank some more of her coffee, nibbled another cookie, and dusted off her fingers before she turned the page.

The light reflected off Layney's charm and caught Bella's attention. She briefly thought of the tear-drop pendant Aerowyn wore in the prologue. She shook it off as coincidence.

She read on, and the library seemed to disappear into a château surrounded by ornate gardens, where summer had faded. The roses began their winter retreat and their pedals shriveled or shed due to the cooler nightly fall temperatures. The trees turned into blazes of golds and reds that complimented the parade of carriages, bringing guests and colorfully costumed acrobats, fire eaters, and jesters.

Bella followed them into a magnificent, opulent ballroom. Men in embroidered satin coats and women with towering wigs and elaborate silk ballgowns milled about the candle-lit room.

Movement drew her attention to a small boy peeking past the long skirts and stockinged legs. His black hair was tousled, and his cheeks flushed. She couldn't help smiling. He'd probably sneaked down from his nursery the way she'd done when Mom and Dad held New Year's parties when she was small. One time, she'd felt so overwhelmed by the people and noise that she'd cried. Poor boy. Bella eased between guests, determined to help him back to his own room.

He huffed out a disappointed breath. Gerard—

Wait. How did she know his name? The ballroom lost some of its clarity before she realized she'd read it. That was right. It was in the book. Still, Gerard? Bella's forehead scrunched. That wasn't a very common name. What were the odds of that?

Even so, this wasn't so bad, not like Layney's claim that she'd been a dragon.

Bella edged closer to the boy, but he was backing out of the room. Maybe he didn't need her after all.

Then, an unusual clickety-clack sound drew her attention from the boy. An old woman dressed in a tattered, gray, hooded cloak wobbled into the ballroom, leaning heavily on a crooked walking stick. The music and conversation halted. The only sound in the room was the elderly woman's steps that echoed against the ballroom walls as the fancily dressed guests gawked at her.

A regal woman in brocade silk and a tall man pushed through the crowd.

For a moment, Bella wondered how she knew the elegant woman was Adalicia, but her confusion lifted even while Adalicia demanded, "Who let you into our home?"

"The guards did," the old woman rasped.

Adalicia addressed her husband, Garren. "You need to punish them for allowing that... thing into our estate." Her face soured as she sneered at the old woman. "This is a private party, and you are not welcome."

"I've been traveling for a long time, and I'm thirsty." The elderly woman's brows furrowed. "I'll be on my way, but could you spare me some water before I leave?"

Garren laughed. "You foolish old woman! This party is for invited guests only. Go ask in the village."

The old woman straightened, and Bella noticed a familiar gold pendant around her neck. Where had she seen it before? The thought slipped out of her head when the old woman's walking stick began to straighten and shrink. Wood became gold topped with a bejeweled sun-shaped design.

A whiff of sulfur made Bella cough.

Behind Bella, the boy yelped, and the men and women around Bella gasped as the woman's ragged clothing transformed into a sparkling lavender gown. The woman's wiry gray hair softened into a golden blonde, and her wrinkled skin flattened into smooth porcelain. Her dull gray eyes flashed into vivid violet. The young enchantress was abnormally beautiful, but somehow her face was familiar.

Bella gaped. She'd just read about—

"I am Aerowyn, the enchantress."

The guests backed away, leaving Adalicia and Garren alone with her in the center of the ballroom.

Aerowyn's words flowed like a violin's music. "I have walked the earth for centuries and have seen many humans' wretched behavior. I see how dreadfully you treat people.

The couple paled, but they didn't look repentant.

"You have set a bad example for your sons. You must change your ways, or they will repeat your sins."

Aerowyn circled her golden scepter into the air, and the odor of sulfur became stronger. A child's light footsteps tapped across the floor, and Gerard walked into the room, his little face pallid in the generous candlelight. The count and countess's eyes widened. A lump of fear formed in Bella's throat as the boy was lifted in the air and forced to join his parents. The enchantress waved her wand again, and all the party guests froze into place like statues—including Bella.

But the prologue! She'd read in the prologue that Aerowyn used her magic for good, hadn't she? Where was the good of this? Bella's palms grew clammy as air gushed out of her lungs.

Gerard grabbed onto his father's coat, and Garren boomed, "I don't know what kind of witchcraft this is"—he pointed at Aerowyn—"but you will undo it and leave."

"Garren and Adalicia," Aerowyn said coldly, "people all over France are starving, barely able to stay alive, while you throw lavish parties. You don't even treat other nobles with kindness. Your behavior is atrocious."

Adalicia raised her chin. "What business is it of yours what we do?"

Aerowyn curled up her lip. "With wealth comes responsibility. You inherited this from your family; you didn't earn it, and you definitely don't deserve it. It is my turn to stop this cycle before your sons grow up to be as arrogant and beastly as you are."

Little Gerard looked up at his father. "Père, what did she mean that people are starving?"

"Get out of our house!" Garren snarled. "Undo your evil magic and get out!"

"Very well. I'll release them when I leave." Aerowyn's eyes narrowed. "But I'm taking Gerard with me. He will be raised by a poor family. Maybe they can teach him some manners and undo your bad example."

Though something still held her frozen like a statue, Bella's heart pounded. Was Aerowyn going to take little Gerard?

The boy pulled at his mother's skirt. His voice squeaked when he said, "Mère?"

The enchantress's voice lost its melodic sound. "I've already given you many chances for redemption. I've entered your lives many times, and at every turn, you treated me deplorably. Giving me water was your last chance for salvation." Aerowyn stomped her foot. "You failed. Wealth is your responsibility, and power is mine. I cannot allow this cycle to continue."

At the mention of power, Adalicia's eyes grew wide. "No…"

"If you don't change your ways, Gerard's twin brother, Antoine, will grow up to be exactly like you." Aerowyn's lips turned downward. "And I will know if Antoine becomes selfish or arrogant. I will test him as I have tested you. He won't be able to escape my wrath if he becomes as beastly as his parents. This is my fair and final warning. If you ignore me, Antoine and his household will suffer even greater than you will."

Garren tried to grab Aerowyn, but she waved her scepter. He froze as well.

"I'll erase him from everyone's memories but yours." The enchantress's voice lost none of its severity as she continued. "You will miss your son until your dying day."

Adalicia fell to the ground in front of Aerowyn, leaving her little boy standing alone. "Please forgive us. We'll change. Don't take Gerard away."

"It's too late for that, but, I will allow one thing." Aerowyn's violet eyes turned brown.

The skin on the back of Bella's neck tingled.

"In your will, you may tell Gerard that you're his parents and bequeath him half of your estate. Until that day, you will be erased from his memory. After you both die, he may know." She stepped over Adalicia, knelt before Gerard and tucked a stray hair behind his ear. "This is my gift to you, Gerard. You will live with a humble and poor family, and that will be your chance to develop a kind heart."

Aerowyn spun her wand, and Gerard's body lifted into the air.

His father bellowed, "No!"

Gerard and Aerowyn disappeared into a sulfurous smelling vapor. Garren and Adalicia stared wide-eyed at the spot where their son had been. Tears welled in Adalicia's eyes, but Garren remained stoic. They said nothing.

Bella scanned the ballroom and the guests were freed from their statue-like state. The shiny floor soon filled with dancing feet and swishing gowns. Everyone, but the count and countess had returned to merriment. The enchantress warned no one would remember Gerard but his parents. Bella observed exchanged glances between the de la Roses—the unspoken conversation. They would not be able to discuss what had occurred only moments before without sounding insane.

Was the story finished? What about Gerard? This book had over a hundred pages to read, but instead of following Gerard, Bella became queasy as the cacophony of instruments turned dissonant. The pleasant strings of violins turned to screeching noises in her head.

With the threat of a migraine coming on, Bella wanted to return to the library, and then go home to sleep it off in the dark. Instead, she was sucked out of the ballroom and put into a space with no color or light.

Chapter 6

Gerard

Gerard startled awake to the sound of his mother calling him to go feed the animals because Father had gone to town to sell the cows. He yawned and woke his younger brothers, but when they moaned, Gerard paid them no mind.

There was too much to be done. His family worked hard. True, they managed to have food on the table, but no matter what they paid, the debts piled higher and higher.

The scent of bread reached the loft and Gerard's stomach grumbled in response, but his mother's words finally breached his sleepiness. He dressed hurriedly and jumped down the ladder.

"Why is Father selling the cows?"

Mother's brows furrowed, but she didn't look up from the bread she was kneading. "We weren't able to pay the rent this month. Father hoped the money from the sale will help appease the landlord. If there is enough left over, he has other debts to pay."

Gerard's shoulder slumped. "He should have told me, Mother. I'm eighteen. I can find a job in town and still help here on the farm in the evenings. The younger ones can help with the easier tasks, but I'll do what I can."

"Don't fret, Son." His mother finally met his eyes and smiled wearily. "We'll figure something out. Eat. Then do your chores."

He obeyed, but all morning, while sweat trickled down his back and gathered around his hairline, Gerard worried. He might not be a son by birth, but he loved his parents, who had taken him in when he was younger than his youngest brother. He couldn't remember life before then. His earliest recollections were of a strange old woman talking to his parents. Even now, in his dim memory, the old woman's eyes were mysterious.

With each new task Gerard pondered over ways to help his parents. After he fed the chickens and pigs, he moved the bundles of hay he had gathered the day before from the fields into the barn. By midday, his muscles ached with fatigue, but Father always said, "If you end up sore after a day of work, that means you accomplished something." There was a level of satisfaction, too, in knowing that he stood taller and broader and could do a man's work.

It was barely afternoon and Father found Gerard in the chicken coop.

"Son, thank you for doing the chores." His smile didn't reach his eyes. "Your mother told me you want to find a job to help out the family."

"Yes." Gerard put the lid on top of the chicken feed barrel.

"There is a wonderful opportunity to serve France that was posted while I was in town. Everyone was talking about it." He sighed heavily. "Don't tell your mother I was the one to give you the idea, because she wouldn't want you to leave home, but it may offer you a better life."

Gerard quirked his head. "What is it?"

"Why don't you go into town and pick up the horse bit I ordered from the blacksmith." He handed Gerard some coins from his pocket. "I purposely forgot it so I wouldn't have to lie to your mother about sending you away." Gerard's father frowned. "I'm leaving out all the details for you to discover to make it look like your idea, but that doesn't mean I'm eager to see you leave." He patted Gerard on the shoulder.

Gerard's curiosity had him hurrying to tidy his hair and sponge off the dirt and sweat with well water. As soon as he felt presentable for town, he headed up the dirt road. He sped up when he saw the small crowd gathered around the news board. It was probably the opportunity Father mentioned. He straightened his collar when he noticed the prettiest girl standing with her father, and for a brief second, they made eye contact. Her lips straightened in disdain. He imagined he wasn't good enough for her. She came from a wealthy family. Gerard looked away. They left, and he peered over the other townsfolk's heads to see the notice that drew everyone's attention.

"What's it say?" one man questioned.

"The French Royal Army is recruiting," Gerard read. "They'll train, feed, and pay us to join."

Gerard's best friend, Leo, sidled up to the crowd.

Gerard shouldered a few men aside so Leo could read the notice too. Since they were children, the shorter boy had allowed everyone to push him around, and Gerard had become his body guard to keep the bullies away.

Gerard glanced down at his friend. "Are you thinking of enlisting?"

Leo nodded. "It would be an answer to my family's problems. I could send them my wages, so they won't lose their home."

It was a good idea. "My family needs the money too. Maybe we could fight in the same unit?"

Leo gave him a half-smile. "It isn't something I want to do. But for my family? I'll sign up."

War was dangerous, but Gerard's heart raced at the thought of adventure. Getting paid to have that kind of fun was *exactly* what he was looking for to help his family. His chest puffed out as he imagined himself in a fine uniform. Maybe he would become the kind of man pretty girls noticed, *and* give his parents the security they deserved at the same time.

Someone exclaimed, "General de la Rose is in charge of the enlistment."

Leo's eyes hardened. "It's his fault my family is in this predicament."

He'd been repeating the same thing for as long as Gerard could remember, so he only said, "I thought he has been living in America for fourteen years."

"He has. I guess the Americans have enlisted his help." Leo added begrudgingly, "He should know how to lead the French. He had served in King Louis's army."

Everyone knew that, so Gerard asked, "Why did he leave France anyway?"

Leo shrugged, but his face still puckered with resentment. "There were a lot of rumors, but no one really knows."

"Now that France is entering the American War with England, I guess his move to Louisiana is beneficial." Gerard stared at the poster.

"I'm not doing this for him." Leo shook his head. "I'll sign up for my family and for France and getting back at the British."

One of the other men added, "We'll crush the English and come home proud."

Gerard hated tyranny and bullies, but what really appealed to him, after taking some of the weight off Father's shoulders, was the vision of medals of valor adorning his uniform. War would earn him the respect he deserved.

This was his destiny.

It didn't take long for Gerard's perspective about war to change. Combat wasn't glamorous. Killing to avoid being killed wasn't heroic. As he and his fellow French soldiers fought alongside the ragtag American army, the goal to survive replaced his dreams of glorious honor. All he wanted was to return home in one piece, but even if he survived, he'd constantly replay the horrors of war.

Despite the coppery smells of injured bodies and the discord of weapons that rung in Gerard's ears even during sleep, he was thankful for the opportunity to support his family, avenge France, and defend freedom.

Then, Leo was wounded, and after Gerard had carried him off the battlefield the doctor said Leo's leg was unsavable. Any infection—the silent enemy of all soldiers—would kill him. As the doctor chopped off Leo's leg, Gerard stayed by his best friend. His screams echoed in Gerard's ears for days. Even in the stillness of the night, the sound haunted him. So did all the other battleground horrors—too many of which he had committed himself.

In order to survive, Gerard built a wall of callousness around his heart. He stopped looking at people as humans. They were enemies to kill or tools to use. The only person he cared about was Leo.

Gerard visited Leo every chance he could in the rudimentary tents for the injured or sick. The odors of rotting flesh mingled with moans and screams, but Gerard wasn't deterred. Leo had been loyal throughout their childhood, and though he'd lost his leg, Gerard wasn't going to add the pain of abandonment to his suffering.

It was during one of Gerard's late afternoon visits that the most beautiful girl he had ever seen walked into the tent. Her golden hair reminded Gerard of wheat fields and her blue eyes put the sky to shame.

Of course, she ignored them. Girls usually did, despite his height and obvious strength.

"Leo," Gerard whispered, "who is that girl?"

"She's a colonist volunteer. She hasn't been here long, only since yesterday, and assists the doctor." Leo glanced at her. "Don't set your heart on her."

They sat in silence a moment until Leo moaned.

Gerard jerked his attention back to his friend. "Are you well?"

"Yes. Stop staring." Leo grunted as he repositioned. "She's not a painting. Also, she's off limits to soldiers."

The swish of skirts and a faint clean floral scent prompted Gerard to partially turn his head. He attempted to face Leo while scanning the area for the woman's location through his peripheral vision. She was changing the wrapping of a soldier two cots over. When she finished, she approached them. Gerard inhaled deeply, but forced himself to look at his friend.

"Excuse me," she said in French with an American accent. Her voice reminded Gerard of music. "I need to change your bandages."

He shifted to the side, and she moved closer to Leo and smiled. "What's your name?"

"Leo," he said through gritted teeth.

"I'll try not to hurt you, Leo, but I will have to lift your limb to get the old bandage off and add the new one." She patted his good foot. "You've been tremendously brave already, but you must be valiant again to prevent infection."

Leo somehow smiled through the pain etched across his face.

"Is there anything I can do to help?" Gerard offered in stilted English, because her accent made it clear to him that she was American.

"You speak English?" When Gerard nodded, she flashed him a smile. "If you could help hold his leg steady. I don't want it to get jostled too much."

Gerard followed her instructions. Any thought of catching her attention was forgotten as Leo went ashen.

"My name is Elayne," she offered, her eyes focused on her task.

Leo's auburn hair moistened with sweat, and Gerard grimaced in empathy.

She tucked the off-white bandages into a basket and moved on.

Gerard stayed at Leo's side until his friend finally drifted into an uneasy rest. Gerard edged between cots toward the exit. He was preoccupied with his friend's pain, and almost bumped into the petite figure in the dark blue cloak.

"Excuse... "

Cornflower-blue eyes met his, and his words faded away.

"You stayed?" Elayne averted her gaze. "For your friend?"

Wordless, he nodded.

She placed a slim hand on his arm. "Don't worry. He is going to live, and that is what matters most. My father lost his leg years ago. He manages quite nicely on his wooden limb. The pain will lessen as he heals."

"I hope so." Gerard smiled weakly. "He's like a brother to me."

She straightened but still had to tilt her head to make eye-contact. "What is your name, soldier?"

"Gerard." Nerves turned his bass voice into a squeaking alto.

She stifled a giggle with her hand, then cast a glance out into the early evening.

"Are you waiting for someone?" He managed to keep his voice deep that time.

A frown pulled at her pretty lips, "Yes, but no one has come. I was supposed to be home before sunset."

Distant cannon fire made her jump.

"I don't mean to presume, but would you escort me home?"

He wiped sweaty palms onto his pants.

Elayne added, "My house is only a few miles away from this camp."

Gerard slightly dipped his head. "I would be honored to accompany you."

They strolled side-by-side close enough to touch. He kept one eye on her and one on the road ahead—always alert in case of an enemy encounter.

Elayne twisted her head up when she spoke to Gerard. Though French wasn't her native language and English wasn't his, they managed to carry on a conversation.

"Where did you learn to speak English?" Even with a simple question, Elayne's words were poetic to Gerard.

"One of the American soldiers taught me."

"You've learned it well. If you didn't have an accent, I would have assumed you were American. Well, except for the uniform." She blushed.

"Where did you learn French?"

"My mother was French." Elayne exhaled. "She died when I was twelve, and Papa never recovered from the loss."

"I'm sorry," Gerard whispered.

"Thank you." She glanced up at him. "That's why I'm here instead of far from the battlefield. I will not leave Papa too."

"My family is in France."

"You must miss them."

"I do." Gerard gulped, silently urging himself to be as honest as she'd been. "Actually, my parents died when I was four, but my mother and father—the couple who took me in—accepted me as their own." Afraid he would see rejection in her eyes, he looked away.

"Oh." She stopped and touched his arm, and when he met her eyes, they were round with sympathy. "I'm so sorry."

"I was fortunate enough to be accepted by my family."

"Papa tries to make up for the absence of Mama as much as he can. I feel blessed." She pulled her cloak closer and said slowly, "It must feel hollow to not remember your parents. It's the memories of my mother that keeps her near my heart. Every time I think I'm going to drown in loneliness, I look up at the stars and think about the stories she told me about them. It brings me comfort to move forward whenever I recall those." Elayne twisted her sun-kissed locks around her fingers. "I miss her fiercely at times, but rather than slip into despair, I stay the course as she would have wanted me to do."

Gerard pondered Elayne's words. "I don't know. I can't miss parents that I can't remember. Life was hard on the farm, and once in a while, I wondered about them or felt a little empty, but I was loved." A tiny smile crossed his face. "That's what matters in the end, isn't it?"

Elayne grasped the pendent that hung on a chain around her neck. "Yes, I agree. I hope to visit France and see where Mama grew up."

"When you finally get to see France, I'm sure you'll love it as I do. The idyllic landscape of rolling hills and meandering rivers provide tranquility in the midst of life's toils." Gerard's smile faltered. "I miss home when I'm..."

They continued for a while in silence. The dusty pathway took the shine out of Gerard's freshly polished boots and turned Elayne's hem brown. The air cooled pleasantly, accenting the scents from the nearby soil and grass field. It reminded Gerard of home. He inhaled the refreshing scent—a reprieve from the odors of war.

"Where exactly are we going?" Gerard perused the area." I thought all civilians had been evacuated for their safety."

Elayne acquiesced. "Since my father is a general, he has nicer quarters. A family who left to avoid being caught in the cross-fire of the war has loaned us their home."

As they talked, however, a pleasant comfort replaced Gerard's initial nervousness.

"Where did you live before the war?" Gerard wanted to know everything about this woman.

"We moved around a lot. Papa's career was partially the reason, but I suspect he also wants to escape reminders of Mama."

Gerard stared at Elayne and saw the same expression Leo had when he lost his leg. He supposed that heartbreak came in a variety of ways and left visible and invisible scars.

Elayne turned her head and Gerard quickly moved his gaze forward. "Where in France did you live?"

"Giverny, a small farm town that's northwest of Paris." Thoughts of home stirred longings for the simpler times, but Gerard's emotions were at a crossroads. He wouldn't exchange this moment with Elayne despite the sadness he felt for leaving his childhood behind.

Elayne hummed, "Do you miss it?"

"Yes, but I'm beginning to understand how discomfort can create growth. Much like when my mother pruned the roses in front of our home. It took cutting away the dead stems for new ones to replace it. I don't enjoy the pruning part of life, but it has led me to meet you for which I'm thankful." Gerard's voice pitched higher and his face warmed because of it.

She sighed. "I know exactly what you're saying. I had to grow up faster than I wanted to when my mother died."

They finally reached Elayne's temporary home, a colonial style brick building with white pillars in front.

Gerard gained confidence from Elayne's kindness and willingness to be open about her personal life. He dared to request, "May we spend more time together in the future?"

She smiled shyly. "Whenever you visit Leo, we can talk then."

He bowed deeply. "Then I will see you as often as I can."

Gerard left Elayne safely ensconced in the beautiful white shingled home, but his thoughts remained on her mesmerizing blue eyes and silken blonde tresses.

He found himself whistling a tune from his childhood as he jogged back down the road.

It was strange how people came into a person's life.

It was extraordinary, too, that in the middle of a war zone, thousands of miles from home, Gerard was falling in love.

Chapter 7

Bellarose

A rotten egg odor surrounded her reminding Bella of the enchantress's spell. Was she still inside the book? The ballroom had disappeared along with the little boy Gerard and the enchantress.

Bella floated as if gravity didn't exist. Where was the ground? Where were the walls? There was no ceiling nor floor. Off to her left side was an illuminated hour glass larger than life turning upside down. It was so bright that it shone on the other objects hovering in mid-air. To her right a gigantic grandfather clock gonged twelve times emitting a painful ringing. She covered her ears in a vain attempt to block the raucous sounds.

A book bigger than the clock danced in front of Bella and the pages whipped quickly. Wind slapped her face tangling her hair in mid-air and pulling on her shirt.

Bile rose in Bella's throat and the hairs on her arms prickled. Since her feet weren't touching anything, her body began to flip and turn faster and faster—Bella was going to be sick.

Conversations with her parents flashed into her mind's eye as reality and fantasy collided.

"Bella, are you listening?" Dad said. "My company was making cuts, and my boss released me from my job."

"Yes, I know, but Daddy, you said yourself it's only a temporary setback." Bellarose glanced between her parents. "It's two weeks to Christmas."

Her dad rubbed his bloodshot eyes. "I know."

"Can't you get another job?"

"I'm looking, Bella, but in the meantime, we have to move."

"What? Where?"

"An apartment."

Bella's mind whirled in disbelief. "Why?"

"It's complicated." Her dad heaved a sigh. "I made some bad investments and your mother and I spent more on this house and our nice things than my job paid. We can't afford to live in this mansion." His eyes welled up. "We don't even own most of our possessions."

"What does that even mean?"

"We didn't pay for our house and things with cash, we borrowed the money. The bank and credit card companies loaned us the money to buy all this." He waved his hand indicating their house and things.

Bella, momentarily struck silent then spoke. "My car?"

Dad nodded.

"What about my bedroom furniture and the desk you gave me last Christmas?"

He nodded again and added, "You can keep your bicycle."

Aghast, she commented, "The stupid childish thing you gave me when I turned thirteen?"

Her parents remained silent.

"What about my books?"

Bella's mother choked out, "You can keep only what fits in one suitcase. They'll be coming to take everything tomorrow." She wiped at tears that made her black mascara run and smudge under her red-rimmed eyes.

"When you say, *they*? You mean the bank and people who own our stuff will be coming?"

"People who work for the bank and creditors, but basically, yes." Her father affirmed.

"You can't be serious! That's not fair!"

"Sometimes life isn't fair, Bella." He turned away. "Go pack. We'll be leaving in the morning." He wasn't going to *cry* in front of her, was he? Bella stiffened. Her dad had always been the parent she knew she could talk to when things went wrong.

Bella stomped away to her room and slammed the door. How could this be happening to her? She couldn't fit her whole wardrobe and library into one suitcase. It was ridiculous that they even suggested it. As she tossed her favorite and practical clothes into the luggage, she assumed her dad would get a similar job and buy her replacements. That was the only thing that helped her leave behind so much. Choosing her favorite books to shove in with her clothes was going to be nearly impossible, but *someday*, those would be replaced too.

Color exploded into the space and the sounds abruptly stopped. Bella stood on a solid wooden surface away from the previous void. Appreciation that she managed to literally keep her cookies down disappeared quickly when the wretched odor of vomit and a new rocking motion brought on more nausea. She regretted eating the delightful snack before opening this book—was she still reading it? Despite the horrible smells, Bella's migraine had miraculously disappeared.

Water slapped a hard surface and a swaying motion gave Bella a flashback of the time she vomited over her dad's business partner's yacht when they had vacationed together.

She pivoted to investigate her surroundings and her breath hitched from the shocking sight of her parents lying on makeshift beds with oozing blisters covering their red feverish faces.

"Bella," her father gasped. "Please get your mother and I some water." He coughed and closed his eyes.

Bella spotted a nearby bucket full of what she hoped was clean water. She scooped the liquid with a wooden ladle attached to the side and slowly carried the cup to her mom's lips. Bella's hand brushed over her mother's ice-cold skin.

"Mom, Mom, wake up!" She shook her mother. "Dad, she isn't waking up." Her father wouldn't open his eyes.

She shook him, but as her mom's body, his was also rigid and remained lifeless.

"No!" The ladle dropped as Bella's throat constricted. "No, this isn't what Layney talked about!"

The room creaked as the floor dipped again. She was on a ship? An old, wooden ship? Bella's stomach knotted.

"I want to leave this story now!" she demanded, but nothing happened. "I said, I want to leave this story! Now!"

Nothing changed as she sat next to her parents' dead bodies.

"I want to leave the story," she whispered in desperation, but still nothing transformed.

Panic grabbed hold of her.

Why couldn't she return to the library? Had the book's magic gone haywire or had Layney lied about everything?

Chapter 8

Gerard

The British attacked more frequently, so several days passed before Gerard had another chance to visit Leo. The previous day's fall rain mucked up his boots, which forced him to clean and polish them. He washed off the past days' grime and shaved, though Leo might tease him for being a dandy. Still, the possibility of seeing Elayne again made him the happiest man in his regiment.

Gerard pushed through the tent's flaps, and a quick glance found Elayne. He had to fight back a grin and found his way to Leo's side. He scanned his friend's injury, then met his eye.

"How are you feeling?"

Leo grunted. "About the same. Where have you been?"

"I've been killing some British soldiers for you."

"Good."

Further conversation tapered off as Elayne approached. Her attention flitted to Gerard, then away. He frowned. She seemed worried, for her brows knitted, and a rush of concern for his oldest friend took hold.

"Leo, let me take a look at your bandages."

She set a basket of fresh wrappings onto a nearby table and then inspected his leg. The white cloth around Leo's stump had some light-yellow discoloration.

"You need new ones," she said quietly.

"Is he—" Gerard swallowed hard. "What can I do?"

Elayne unwrapped the amputated limb and let out a soft breath.

"Thankfully, I see no sign of an infection. Gerard, could you fetch me a basin of water." She pointed to a table near the back of the tent. "I want to clean this before I put on new bandages."

"Of course." Gerard turned at once, though a sliver of doubt edged into his thoughts.

Was Elayne paying special attention to Leo? Had she been the only one to assist Leo?

He wrestled his mind under control and brought her the basin. She dipped a clean cloth into it and gently wiped Leo's stump.

"So," Elayne said in English, "Leo, were you two friends before you came to America?"

Leo shuddered, glanced up at Gerard, who repeated the question in French, and answered, "We met when we were four."

"Four?" She raised her eyebrows. "That's a long time to stay friends. My papa moved me around too much to make friends, and I have but a few."

"Leo was there for me when I lost my parents." Gerard straightened but put on a smile for them both. "If you can believe it, he was taller than me back then."

"True." Leo's grimace turned to a tight-lipped smile. "He had an unusual growth spurt when we turned thirteen. I'm not really that short. Gerard is abnormally tall."

Elayne finished and looked up at Gerard. "Leo is my last patient. Do you have time to stay and talk?"

He bowed. "Of course!"

"Let me wash my hands." Elayne moved to the nearby basin of clean water and thoroughly scrubbed.

When she returned, she requested of Gerard, "Would you sit down?"

He grabbed the chair, and the next few moments were among the best he had experienced in America, barring only walking alone with Elayne. The three of them talked of their childhoods and life before the war, of favorite things and gentler memories. Although Leo needed Gerard to interpret some of what Elayne said, they all enjoyed each other's company.

Every chance Gerard had, he slipped to the tents to visit Leo and to see Elayne, who always seemed present. The time together grounded Gerard. Leo smiled more. Even Elayne seemed joyful when the three of them talked, which made Gerard even happier.

War was no longer an adventure for glory-seekers, but Gerard fought bravely against the British, achieving respect from his fellow soldiers. The longer he fought, though, the more he wanted an end to the fighting. The possibility of a future with a beautiful young woman was more compelling than acclaim had been.

Then, one day after an especially hard skirmish, General de la Rose approached Gerard. "Your bravery on the battlefield is honorable. Your family would be proud of your courage."

The general didn't linger, but Gerard's ego puffed a little. The accolade simmered inside him with bursting excitement, and he *had* to tell someone. That evening, he forwent cleanup and rushed to the hospital tents, where Elayne had just finished changing Leo's bandages. He could barely contain himself.

"Good day," he said, grinning from ear to ear.

Leo squinted. "What has you so cheerful?"

"Gerard!" Elayne pointed to the splatters on his uniform. "I hope none of that blood is yours."

"Of course not." Gerard threw back his shoulders and announced, "General de la Rose gave me a high compliment for my bravery today."

Leo frowned at the general's name.

Elayne raised her eyebrows. "Oh really, and what was that?"

Their lack of enthusiasm squelched some of his zeal, but he shared, "He said my bravery on the battlefield was honorable and that my family should be proud of me."

Leo crossed his arms and stared past Gerard at the tent's canvas wall.

Elayne clasped her hands on her lap. "Everyone who fights in a war must be brave to some degree, and I don't doubt that your family in France is proud of you. I know they must value your sacrifice of leaving to help provide for them." She peeked up at him, then her gaze dropped. "I can't—I don't want to hear how you risked your life. Or that you took someone else's."

For a moment, his jaw tightened, then her words sank into his heart. Did she mean that she didn't want to know he was in danger?

"You're only a man," she murmured. "Not immortal. You and the British have blood, bones, muscles, and the ability to die. I don't..."

Remorse overtook his pride.

Here he was bragging about killing men while his friend lay in agony because of his amputated leg. And death would mean leaving Elayne.

"Please," she spoke softly, "be careful. Don't seek glory."

Gerard bowed his head and said, "As you wish, mon ange."

After she exited the tent, Leo quietly admitted, "I want to hear about your victories, but leave out anything about that louse general. I'm really proud of you."

Gerard glanced after Elayne. "But not if it will bother her."

Leo sank back. "No. I guess not."

Elayne reappeared when Gerard stood to leave. "Would..." She hesitated prettily. "Would you walk me home? My chaperone was preoccupied."

His palms sweated.

"Of course he will," Leo put in before Gerard could answer. He winked at Gerard, whose cheeks heated.

They said an awkward goodnight and left. Gerard's heart raced like a frightened rabbit. He and Elayne hadn't been alone since the first day he had escorted her home.

The golden sun set quickly over the pink and blue horizon, and the air held a cool crispness. Darkness soon covered the camp. Gunshots, cannons, and war cries were temporarily quiet as each side settled in for the evening. Camp fire smoke with scents of roasted hare and deer wafted into the air but were soon replaced with woodsy odors of pine trees lining the path.

Elayne shivered and hugged her chest.

"Would you like my jacket, *mon ange*?" Gerard asked.

"If you don't mind," she said. "I forgot my cloak this morning, and lost track of time."

Gerard wrapped his uniform coat around her and it had been so tempting to settle a kiss on her forehead.

"I don't like walking home alone in the dark," she explained.

"I'll walk with you anywhere you ask." Gerard gazed down onto her golden hair that glowed halo-like in the moonlight. Angelic. Elayne looked celestial, but telling her how he felt might ruin what they already had.

The moonlight caught the gold pendent she always wore and made it shimmer against her chest.

If he didn't say something to break the mood, he'd kiss her. "Did someone special give you that necklace you always wear?"

"It was my mother's," she said slowly. "I never take it off in memory of her."

Gerard exhaled in relief and blurted, "I'm glad it isn't from a lost love."

The melancholy expression on her face melted into a coquettish grin. "Why is that?"

And suddenly, he knew it was all right to ask. "Because I was hoping your heart was free. Have you made promises to love another?"

She shook her head. "No."

They walked a few more paces, and she asked, "Gerard?"

"Yes?"

"Does *mon ange* mean my angel in French?"

"*Oui,*"

She slanted her head upward. "Why do you call me your angel?"

That was an easy answer. "You protect me from my own arrogance. You shelter my soul from the horrible things I see and do on the battle-field."

Elayne stopped walking and turned to him. Their eyes met.

"When I could be lost to the darkness war exposes," he continued, his voice hoarse, "you rescue me from the worst of it. Sometimes I fear that if you didn't center me, I would turn into a monster. A beast."

Elayne's eyes welled up. "You give me too much credit. What about Leo?"

"Leo is my best friend, but he doesn't have the inner strength that you do. He can't ward off my worst self." Gerard's heart thumped hard against his chest. He paused to catch his breath then his courage rose.

"As you've said, I'm a man with blood, bones, muscles, and the ability to die. Though I bleed like every other man, I pray that I'm not just any man to you. I hope to be the man you love someday, because you already have my heart, *mon amour*."

Elayne reached outside the enveloping jacket to touch Gerard's arm.

"You already are that man to me."

She tilted her chin upward. Gerard leaned down, and she stood on the tip of her toes. Their lips met.

Elayne loved him.

This was all Gerard would ever need, and someday, when the war was done, he would marry her and take her home to France.

Gerard had escorted Elayne safely home, but his walk back was a blur as he replayed their kiss multiple times, reliving the softness of her lips and the beauty in her eyes.

Even though he was exhausted, Gerard tossed and turned on his narrow cot. Nightmares of explosions inside the camp haunted him all night. A war zone was never safe, but he had to trust that Leo and Elayne were. The euphoria from the night before faded as he was reminded of the dangers of a battleground.

In the morning, he absent-mindedly dressed in his battle-ready uniform, but it hadn't even been a full ten minutes after he stomped on his boots when an explosion boomed in the distance. That was too close. Armed and ready, he dashed from his quarters.

A young man bumped into him, nearly knocking him down. "Sorry, sir! But, it's the British! They advanced during the night!"

Gerard squinted through the smoke and choked as it filled his lungs. Another deafening burst sounded, and cannonballs struck the hospital. Smoke and dust rose into the morning air.

Leo! Elayne! Panic constricted his throat, and he gasped to breathe.

The British didn't have long-range artillery. Gerard spun around.

There. Through the smoke, British soldiers were loading a cannon again. Anger fueled Gerard's sprint. He raised his musket and bludgeoned his enemy's head. Turning, Gerard spun his gun around and shot the soldier manning the cannon. Crimson and flesh colors splattered Gerard's uniform. Undeterred, he bayoneted the loader and two other men. Red oozed from their chests before they could raise their rifles at Gerard.

Unconcerned about danger and the balls whizzing past him, Gerard pivoted and sprinted toward the hospital fire, never looking back, Ahead, the tent blazed with orange and yellow flames. His chest thudded violently. If Leo and Elayne were in there...

He held his collar over his mouth as he searched for Leo. There he was crawling from the rolling smoke. Relief washed over Gerard. Effortlessly, he carried Leo to safety and returned to transport more patients away from the fire.

Despite the inferno, Gerard went back over and over to haul out one man after another to safety. He didn't bother checking if the men he rescued were dead or alive. His leaden chest heaved as he coughed and gagged on smoke, but terror for Elayne kept him moving. *Where was she?*

He twisted around to go back, and two of Gerard's comrades grabbed his arms.

"No! You can't! It's a death-trap!"

He tugged to get loose from their grasps. "Elayne! Elayne!"

"Who?"

"The pretty nurse. She may have escaped," the other one shouted over the chaos.

Gerard's strength gave out, and he collapsed onto the ground.

The first man knelt beside him. "We'll look around the grounds to see if someone pulled her out."

"Or perhaps she's caring for the wounded." The second man suggested.

Gerard nodded. Though his long legs wobbled when he stood, he staggered to where bodies lay. Feeble movement testified that many were still alive and doctors treated burns and additional injuries. Others, however remained motionless.

"Elayne? Elayne!" Gerard wiped at his smoke-singed eyes. "Elayne, are you here?"

She didn't answer.

Gerard continued frantically searching bodies, wandering through rows of injured soldiers and nurses. Desperation kept him going when he was almost too tired to stand. He rolled unconscious or dead bodies face up if they, too, had golden hair. Uniformed men, burned beyond recognition made his stomach heave, and when a familiar skirt peeked out from a blanket, he rushed to uncover the form with a shaking hand. At the sight of the woman's brown hair, he sighed in relief, then berated himself. This must be another soldier's sweetheart.

Then, at the end of the row, Elayne lay, like a sleeping angel, crimson staining her bodice. He rushed forward and dropped to his knees, hesitating for only a second before pulling her into an embrace. His body shook and silent sobs stuck inside his throat. He pressed his lips to her forehead and rocked back and forth.

A thick hand grabbed his coat, and he flung it away. It wrapped around his wrist, and he finally looked over. Lying next to Elayne was General de la Rose.

"Gerard," he somehow gasped, though he was barely breathing. "Gerard, I'm dying."

Gerard didn't loosen his grip on Elayne, but he met the general's unfocused stare.

The man pulled a letter from his jacket's inner pocket. "Please take this. I-it is for you. Only you." His eyes shut, and his breathing stopped.

The letter dropped into Gerard's palm.

Too overcome by Elayne's death to question why the general's dying wish was for Gerard to have a letter, he hastily stuffed the parchment into his pocket. For uncounted minutes, he crouched there, holding Elayne to his heart.

A cannonball hit the ground nearby, spewing dirt and rocks. A call for help sounded behind him, and though it wrenched his heart in two, he couldn't help Elayne. Gerard gently kissed her cold forehead and wiped spatter from her cheek. He laid her on the ground and folded her hands over her heart.

He should have said, "I love you," but it felt wrong to make the confession here, among the dead. She knew. She must have known.

He stood and squared his shoulders. Anger supplanted every other emotion. Gerard walked away, determined to kill every last red coat he could find.

Chapter 9

Bellarose

Instead of returning to the warm, cozy library, the space around her became a port of entry. The line between fiction and reality blurred the longer Bella lived within the story. It was more difficult to remember the world she left while tentatively exiting the ship with wobbly sea legs unaccustomed to the solid ground. The wooden ramp creaked as she inhaled a deep breath. Though the docks briny smells weren't the clean scents of home, they were much improved from the bowels of the ship.

A captain's booming commands and horses' clopping hooves surrounded Bella with a whirl of activity. The bustling commerce of people buying and selling on the streets caught Bella's attention as she noticed a sign overhead 'Welcome to New Orleans' with different sized buildings behind it. Did she know Father had bought a ship passage to Louisiana? How could she have forgotten that detail?

Fear, loneliness, and a wool cloak wrapped around her as she faced the unfamiliar city. She had nothing but a bundled bedsheet containing one dress, a thin nightgown and two books. With the pandemonium of battling emotions, Bella forced her gumption to dominate. She would find a way to survive or die trying.

Bella tentatively strolled toward town. A group of unwashed sailors whistled suggestively.

"Hey pretty girl. Are ye lost?"

She quickened her pace and almost bumped into a young man who was bent over with a hunched back. He wouldn't look her in the eye as he said, "Pardon me, Miss."

His handsome face and reddish, brown hair seemed familiar as a flash of a similar boy who wore glasses faded quickly in her mind's eye.

"Watch ye step, Mutant!" The unsavory sailor spit out to the deformed young man.

The comment made Bella fume.

"I should have been the one to pardon myself," she said loud enough for the rude man to hear. "I wasn't looking where I was going." Then she whispered, "I was trying to get away from those men."

The young man's chocolate brown eyes met hers. "Are those men bothering you?" He pulled out a knife.

Bella gasped, "No, put that away. I was only trying to avoid them since they showed interest in me."

His kind brown eyes met hers and she immediately felt he was someone she could trust.

"It's not safe around here for a young woman to be alone." He straightened slightly. "Where is your chaperone?"

The grief of her parent's death flooded her and she couldn't hold back the tears.

Bella sobbed out, "They died during the voyage."

Eyes were on them and Bella knew she needed to control her emotions. She quickly wiped the tears away on her sleeve and whispered, "My parents died and I have no money. I need a job and a place to stay."

"I can help you with that." His smile was comforting. "Follow me and I'll keep you from getting hassled or harmed."

Bella pulled up her skirt slightly and walked next to the young man. He seemed shy, but pleasant. "What's your name? I'm Bellarose Bonnay, but you can call me Bella."

He tilted his head to the side to address her. "I'm Quinn." It was laborious for him to walk and look at her so he turned his neck toward the path. "My father owns a tavern and if you don't mind serving drinks and food to people, he will allow you to stay at his inn above the pub."

Bella immediately panicked. She didn't know how to do anything but read and play the piano. "I'm thankful for the offer, but I'm... not experienced with service type work."

Quinn responded, "Don't worry, I'm sure the other bar maids can teach you. Father won't want to do me any favors, but he likes pretty girls working in his establishment."

Did he just admit she was pretty? Bella's face warmed and Quinn seemed to be blushing.

He cleared his throat. "Um, I mean... I'm sure Father will give you a chance to work for him."

Bella was thankful she literally ran into this boy, because he had become her hero in more ways than one. She didn't have time to wallow in grief and she didn't have any skills to keep safe on the wild streets of New Orleans.

"You don't even know me. Why are you helping me?" She wiped at her eyes as tears threatened to fall again.

"I've felt the despair I saw written on your face back there." He pointed his thumb behind him. "I knew you needed rescuing immediately."

People they approached moved to the opposite side of the street. The expressions were between fear and disgust. Bella wasn't sure if it was because of Quinn or her state of disrepair. It didn't matter because this young man showed her kindness when no one else would, and she was indebted to him.

After they walked for about thirty minutes, they stopped in front of a building with a wooden sign protruding toward the street above the entrance. Engraved on the board were the words 'The Swan' with a picture of the bird and an ale mug.

"This is it. I'm not allowed inside, but I work in the adjoining stables around the back." He pointed in the general direction. "I'm a blacksmith and horse groomer. Whenever you can come visit me," he lowered his voice, "I'll teach you how to use a sword for defense. I believe a single woman should have those skills in this town."

He blushed again, and Bella wasn't sure what she needed, but if the leers from the men at the docks were any indication of how she would be treated, perhaps learning how to protect herself wasn't a bad idea.

"Thank you. I will come to you for lessons once I figure out what I'm doing." She looked inside the door. "How do I go about getting a job here?"

"Ask for Gustave, that's my father, and tell him you are willing to work for room and board. Tell him someone suggested you come here for a job since you lost your parents on the journey here." He clenched his fists. "Don't mention me, but I think if you smile like you did back there, he'll hire you." Quinn hobbled toward the stables with a genuine grin.

Bella held her breath temporarily and then exhaled.

I can do this. I don't have a choice, she thought as she walked inside The Swan.

Chapter 10

Gerard

The war continued for weeks after Elayne's death, but when all seemed hopeless, the Americans finally gained their victory. French soldiers began returning home with stories of glory and conquest to share with families and friends in France, but victory didn't matter to Gerard. Elayne was dead, and he no longer loved life.

Gerard didn't follow his fellow Frenchmen home. Leo needed to recover before a long sea voyage, so Gerard decided to stay with him. They went with their company down to New Orleans, where he found a room above a tavern called The Swan. After he relocated their sparse belongings in the lodgings, he and Leo slowly made their way to the docks to bid their fellow Frenchmen farewell.

Leo's face was beaded with sweat before long, and Gerard slowed.

"I can make it," Leo ground out.

"Hmm? Oh, yes," Gerard answered, trying to make it seem as if he were studying the buildings around them instead of easing his pace out of consideration for his friend. "Of course you can. I was only thinking."

"About?"

"It's nice to be in an ordinary town again."

Leo nodded understanding, evidently sharing his relief that the commonplace town was far enough from the ravages of war, thus avoiding constant reminders.

One of the French lieutenants raised his voice, and the soldiers quieted. "During that last battle," he said, "one man stood above the rest. I do not refer to his height, but to his actions. To his bravery, valor, and courage. Gerard!"

Gerard startled. "Sir?"

"Come up here."

Leo nudged him to go forward. The crowd parted to let him through, and he looked at his boots, to avoid eye-contact. He was no hero. His courage was born of emptiness—he had nothing to live for.

After the British had killed his beloved, Gerard lost control as he sought to obliterate the enemy. He pursued each redcoat with vehemence, and in his wake, he unnecessarily mutilated them. Risks meant nothing. Gerard wanted to die and take the British army with him. The fact that he continued to breathe only worsened his lust for revenge. On the field, he was barely human—a beast—but others overlooked Gerard's atrocities because he was always victorious.

When the lieutenant finished his speech, Leo patted Gerard on the back. "The accolades couldn't be for a better person!"

Gerard smiled with a closed mouth—he didn't deserve the praise.

Leo was still pale, so Gerard made a show of celebrating his recognition and hired a carriage to take them both home. He left Leo in the tavern and trudged up the stairs. For a long time, he stared at the wall. How very different this was than he had hoped.

Finally, he crossed to the wardrobe and unpacked their meager belongings. Deep in a neglected pocket, he found the blood splattered letter that General de la Rose had given him. The wrinkled paper brought back the bone-deep horror, and he shuddered and tucked it away. He had enough to worry about now. He'd deal with it later.

The wooden floor suddenly turned crimson underneath his feet and the coppery odor of blood choked him. The doorway was blocked by piles of dead British soldiers he had killed. Gerard rubbed his eyes and the images disappeared.

He stumbled down the stairs and ignored Leo to catch fresh air out in the alley near The Swan. An apparition of Elayne stood in front of him. He reached out to touch her face, but she evaporated into thin-air. His hands shook and sweat formed on his brow.

This wasn't the only time images of his love appeared after being surrounded by bloodied bodies, and each time the hallucinations fooled him. Gerard was wearied by the repeated imaginary visions his mind conjured up during the day or in the darkness.

The following evening before dawn, night terrors drenched him in sweat as morbid thoughts threatened to run amok while they spilled over into his nightmares.

He tried to escape them with thoughts of Elayne—his bright ray of light, but Elayne turned on him. "Everyone has the capability for both evil and good, but you chose evil."

Gerard cried out, "But pain has reconstructed the landscape of my soul."

Elayne glared at him and warned, "Don't let the inner demons win."

Before Gerard could say anything else, she gave him the same cold blank stare as when she died then her body turned into mist.

Gerard jerked awake.

Leo's perky voice called out, "Good morning, Gerard!"

Gerard grumbled, "What's so good about it?"

"We're alive and I bet there are some new people waiting to hear how amazing you were on the battlefield." Leo pushed himself up from the bed with gritted teeth. "You'll get more free drinks and the bar maids will swoon over you."

"Yes, but Elayne is still dead and nothing can fix that."

Leo frowned, but hopped over with his crutch to Gerard. He patted his arm. "Come on. We have to eat and perhaps today will bring new patrons into The Swan. I hope to find someone who will give me a job."

Gerard helped Leo down the stairs to the tavern, where they ate a hearty breakfast. They had money from their service in the French army, but that would run out soon.

Gustave, the tavern owner, plopped a mug in front of Leo, then pushed another to Gerard. The pale brew sloshed onto the table.

Carefully avoiding the puddle, Gerard took a swig. "Gustave, do you know of anyone hiring?"

"I'll ask around." Gustave rubbed his pointy chin. "I'm sure there would be more than one willing to hire a war hero like ye-self."

Leo gulped up the ale and let out, "Aww! That's mighty tasty." He swiped his sleeve over his face. "I'll need a job too once I'm healed."

Gustave looked disdainfully at Leo, "Aye, I'm sure if I tell them you're Gerard's friend that will help."

Leo frowned, but a plate full of fried eggs, sausage, and bread provided a welcome diversion. He took a taste, then smiled. "This is good stuff!"

With a crisp nod, the tavern owner trotted off.

Gerard picked at his plate and scowled after Gustave. He didn't like the sneer on the tavern owner's face, but at least the food put Leo back into his normal chipper mood.

Leo had been healing slowly. Gerard had learned of a man who fashioned wooden legs, and once Leo's stump was completely healed, he could get one. At least Leo didn't wince in pain anymore.

"Aren't you going to eat?"

Gerard's attention snapped back to his friend.

"Your food," Leo waved a knife at Gerard's full plate, but the teasing look fled his face.

New patrons sat nearby and Leo started to brag, "Here is a genuine war hero." He pointed to Gerard. "He killed twenty British with his bare hands!"

Leo looked at Gerard as the two men stared wide-eyed at them. Gerard flashed his fake smile that didn't reach his mood and played along with Leo's game as he did every day.

"Leo, get the story straight, it wasn't my bare hands. I had a rifle, and there were at least twenty-five soldiers." Gerard gave a toothy grin.

Laughter erupted from those who heard Gerard's exaggeration.

Gerard whispered, "You don't need to tell everyone who enters the tavern about me."

"Yes, I do." Leo winked. "I'm proud to be your friend, it gets us free ale, and some of the pretty girls are looking at me too."

"I suppose those are the benefits." Gerard shuffled his mug around. "At least I have something to smile about when you're touting over my acts of heroism."

Leo looked at him gravely. "Anything to distract you from despair."

"I know I've seemed inconsolable at times, but I'll play along since it gives you joy." Gerard straightened. "I may be beginning to believe all the stories you tell about me."

"Most of them are true. I only add a little flourish to entertain." Leo held up his mug and shouted, "Give the people what they want!"

The men in the pub yelled, "Huzzah!"

It was easier for Gerard to push away the dark-side whenever he lapped up Leo's flattery and it didn't hurt when The Swan's patrons soaked up the words like parched soil drinks in water.

Leo shouted, "Buy us some ale and I'll tell you how Gerard saved my life from a burning inferno."

Gerard puffed out his chest as his friend weaved the tale and added exaggerated details whenever prompted. Elayne would have criticized the boasts of killing men, but she was dead and it prevented Gerard from turning into a beast.

Chapter 11

Bellarose

B ella wiped the spilt ale from the bar with her old rag as she overheard the little red-haired man brag about his friend. She couldn't help but glance at the tall dark and handsome person, the subject of all the war stories in The Swan.

She swallowed hard, *Why does he look familiar? In my memory, he doesn't belong here but...*

"Bella! Bring these mugs to Gerard and Leo, and don't spill any!" Gustave brusquely commanded as he held out two full steins.

Bella had accidently splashed drinks onto one of the patrons, and Gustave never forgot.

She asked quietly, "Who are Leo and Gerard?"

Gustave's face puckered as he pointed to the muscular man, she thought she recognized. Then images of pages from an oversized book flapped rapidly inside her head. She shook off the strange mind picture when she heard Adele, another bar maid, giggle.

"Everyone knows who dreamy Gerard is. You really are bad at this job."

Bella blushed and took the mugs to the table. She served from behind the men to avoid them seeing her. Adele would have flirted with Gerard and rubbed his shoulder, but Bella wanted to be invisible.

She quickly disappeared into the kitchen where she swept the floor to avoid people. This was where she exited the pub to visit Quinn in the stables, but only when Gustave gave her a break.

"Bella, come out here!" Gustave yelled. "The customers need to be served more and that floor needs sweeping."

She scuffled out in her borrowed shoes. Bella cringed when a black-toothed customer grinned at her after she dropped off his plate of fried fish. He smacked her behind and she scowled at him, but hustled away.

Bella mumbled, "I forgot."

"What did ye forget?" The lecherous man croaked.

She ignored him. She had encountered the presumptuous patron before and tried to serve him in a way he couldn't reach her, but was distracted by Gerard and thinking he came from another life.

"Bella there are more customers to serve!" Gustave interrupted her ponderings and she didn't have time to stop and think for the next hour.

The whole experience at The Swan was trial by fire, and Bella hated it. She didn't like the customers and Gustave was a tyrant. She struggled to see any resemblance between him and his son, Quinn, who was kind and had a pleasant face. She deduced he must have taken after his mother because Gustave's pointed chin resembled a witch's. He could have come straight out of one of her childhood books about Hansel and Gretel.

Books? She had a library full of them at her old house, but where was that? Her memory fogged when she tried to remember her childhood abode.

Thankfully she dodged being spotted by Gerard because he was always surrounded by admiring fans. She carried heavy trays of food and mugs of ale until her arms shook from the strain. Adele left most of the work to Bella, while she flirted with the customers.

"Hey handsome. You look thirsty. Bella, pour me another ale for this attractive gentleman." Adele waved her hand.

The greasy haired man ogled Adele. "Aw shucks. I don't know if I should drink any more. I have an early morning tomorrow."

"Nonsense. With those burly arms," Adele rubbed the man's biceps, "I can see you're a hard worker and deserve a little reward."

Bella's skinned crawled over the exchange, but she obeyed Adele who always succeeded in coaxing already drunk men into ordering more. Gustave wanted the bar maids to encourage the patrons to drink, but she wasn't able to charm men who disgusted her. If she could get away with Adele doing the convincing while she fetched the spirits, Bella wasn't going to complain.

She scraped the leftovers from the plates of the last patron into a bucket. The edible scraps were fed to the pigs, and it was Bella's job to bring it to them.

Outside the black star-studded sky gave her pause. Even with a gloomy life, beauty still existed. Bella didn't dare walk the extra steps in search for Quinn because there were still dishes to be cleaned, but she hoped he was having a better day than she was. Passing thoughts of him brightened her mood a smidgen.

Once everything was clean, Bella trudged up the inn stairs to the room she shared with Adele. Her feet screamed in pain, but she quickened her pace to avoid the risk of running into Gerard since he also stayed in the inn. She couldn't explain her desire to avoid the war hero, but as she tried to pull out memories of where she had seen him before, she drew a blank. From all the rumors and tales about him, she knew he came from France. Maybe she knew him from when she was rich, but he didn't appear to be wealthy.

Adeles snores greeted Bella at the door, but she was bone tired. Nothing would prevent her from falling fast asleep.

The nightmares of her parents' deaths stopped once she started working at The Swan. Exhaustion put her into a deep, dreamless night. Bella was learning to appreciate the small blessings now that she was penniless. If the only joys she could find in this dismal life were Quinn's smiles, diamond filled skies, and dreamless nights, Bella would hold onto them with a firm grip.

Chapter 12

Gerard

Months after the war's end, the British had been forced out of the colonies. Peace and reconstruction filled New Orleans.

"Do you regret not returning to France?" Leo rubbed his stump before putting on his pants.

Gerard shook his head. "No..." He stared off into space, but then continued, "It's not that I don't miss my family, but I needed a change from that life."

Leo nodded silently. He had the same harsh circumstances in France as Gerard and with Louisiana's blend of French, Spanish, Creole, and other cultures, New Orleans was beginning to feel like home.

A knock interrupted their ponderings.

"Here's a package for you all the way from France!" A dirt smudged boy handed Gerard the brown wrapped parcel after he opened the door. The boy stared up at Gerard with admiration and Gerard dug a coin out of his pocket for the boy.

"No payment is necessary. Me friends and I fought to see who would have the honor to meet ye and I won." The boy's wide-mouthed grin displayed two missing front teeth.

Gerard ruffled the boy's hair. "Thank you for bringing it to me unharmed."

The boy walked away backwards still staring up at Gerard until the door was closed.

"It's been twelve weeks since the soldiers left. Maybe our families finally got our letters." Leo eyed Gerard's delivery. "Well, are you going to open it?"

Gerard tore off the brown paper and opened the small box. Inside were two letters and some gold coins.

"Here, this one is for you." Gerard gave Leo the letter with his name scrawled on the outside.

Then he unfolded the one with his own name and read it silently.

Dear Gerard,

It was bittersweet to hear that you're staying in Louisiana, but your mother and I are thankful you're healthy and finding your way in the world. Don't worry about us, because after King Louis was informed of your heroism, he rewarded you with enough gold to pay off the family debt. I included what was left in this package. I was insured that this would reach you undisturbed by a trusted officer of the ship returning to Louisiana."

All our love,

Father

The heaviness lifted from Gerard's chest knowing his family would be all right with his decision. He still needed a way to earn a living but this would help him and Leo until they found something that suited them.

Leo grinned. "My family is doing well. Your father said King Louis was impressed by our heroism and paid off both our families' debts." Leo looked down at his stump. "I guess I'm considered a hero too after losing this leg for France."

Gerard put the gold into a padlocked chest. "Between the visitors to The Swan who pay us with food and drink to hear war stories, and this gold, we don't need to rush into finding jobs."

Leo guffawed. "Today is a good day! With my talent for adding flourishes about your heroics, and the King's reward, I think we're going to survive." Then Leo cleared his throat. "I know we don't need to worry about paying for room and board, but then I met Louise, and she's interested in me and..."

"And?"

"I want to be able to fend for myself, court a girl, get married, and have a family someday." Leo fidgeted with his crutch. "I can't do that living in your shadow. I will be looking for a place to work and move out of The Swan."

Gerard nodded. "I understand and will not be upset when you finally leave. I will someday need to move too. Reliving each battle through your stories isn't always pleasant." Gerard stared down at his feet.

Leo grunted as he hobbled to the door. "Well then, it's settled."

Accounts of Gerard's deeds and the king's favor spread through the city and beyond. The tall yarns were more fantasy than fact, but Gerard reveled in it. In fact, he began to believe all the extraordinary things people said about him.

Leo went out of his way to treat Gerard like a king. Since Leo spoke in French, other tavern patrons interpreted Gerard's conquests, and each anecdote changed slightly as different people relayed Leo's embellished tales.

One night, which began as so many others had, somehow felt different, and Gerard couldn't tell why. Maybe it was because Leo was late, but he still sat on the same stool and spun his stories loudly for all to hear.

"There were many battles, but the one I remember most was when Gerard killed fifty British soldiers with only his knife." Leo stabbed the air, but his imaginary strokes seemed less enthusiastic than usual. "He didn't even break a sweat."

Arms crossed, Gerard leaned back and frowned. Usually, Leo relayed how he'd witnessed the deaths of a hundred men. Despite the story, someone clapped Gerard on the back and handed him a tankard of ale, and he forced a smile of mock humility onto his face. He'd talk to Leo about diminishing his feats later.

For a moment, he could almost see Elayne before him, sadness in her sky-blue eyes.

Gerard gulped the ale to push the memory away.

"That true?" asked the stranger who'd handed him the tankard.

"Well, I won't argue," he answered glibly, taking another swallow to help the inferred lies slip out easier, "though, the way I remember it, fifty was too few."

A cheer went up.

"Leo is wrong about one thing, though. I think I did sweat a little. Killing redcoats is still work."

The room roared in laughter.

"But Leo left out the most important part." Gerard paused until a man called him to continue, so he grinned. "There were a dozen patriot girls swooning over my bravery."

Two rushed up to keep his mug full, and the crowd laughed again.

In a low voice he said, "Ladies, don't argue over me. I can drink all you want to bring me—keep it coming." He winked at the bar maids and the girls just about swooned.

Elayne's voice repeated in his mind, scolding him for his false generosity. He couldn't escape her. He saw her in his nightmares and was reminded of her when he was awake.

He clenched his jaw, shoved the memory away, and said, "See? I could have taken one of the wenches as my wife if I had wanted to. But, why be tied down to one woman for the rest of my life when there are so many to experience?"

He finished the ale as the men cheered.

Leo shook his head and sighed. "I don't know how you do it. Every unmarried woman in town wants you, and you manage to keep them wanting more without making any promises." He looked around nervously. "I've only managed to attract one girl, but Louise is enough for me. In fact, I think she's the one."

Gerard laughed. "Are you going to marry her?"

"She's kind and loves me despite my missing leg." Leo rubbed his thigh. "I didn't mention this earlier, but her father owns the mercantile and asked me to come work for him. He offered me room and board."

"When will you move?" Gerard pushed away the mixture of emotions over this abrupt news.

"Tomorrow." Leo moved his stein around.

"Why did you wait to tell me?"

"I worried about you being lonely, and I know you have nightmares about Elayne, because you yell out in your sleep." Leo wouldn't make eye contact.

Instead of acknowledging his weakness Gerard laughed it off. "I'm going to be splendid. Since I'm not going to get tied down to anyone, your presence will be a hinderance if I want alone time with a wench." Again, Elayne flashed in and out of his memory. He waved his tankard to get a bar maid's attention. "With so many women ready to fill my mug with ale and feed my ego, I will be perfectly fine without you." He chuckled. "I'd be doing the world a disservice if I got married. All those other females would lose the privilege of flattering me."

Leo clapped Gerard on the back. "They'll be writing songs about you someday. Singing about how no one is as great as Gerard and my story telling will be unnecessary."

With that Leo stood up. "Speaking of women, Louise is expecting me at her parent's house for dinner. I must bid you Adieu."

Leo bowed slightly and pivoted toward the door.

"I'll help you move your things tomorrow." Gerard waved.

He wanted the best for Leo, but he wasn't going to enjoy the solitude where painful memories would run amok without Leo's interruptions or cheery comments.

An unfamiliar barmaid caught Gerard's eye as she edged past Leo when he exited. Clear skin, green eyes and brown hair. She was definitely prettier than the other girls. Gerard set down his mug in anticipation of her attention as she gathered empty cups and pushed forsaken chairs under the table.

She also ignored Gerard like he was invisible—something he was no longer accustomed to and didn't like.

The book, sticking out of her apron pocket, caught Gerard's attention, so he grabbed it.

"Give that back!"

"*The Scorned Fae*? Is this any good?" He leafed through the pages and gave her a flirtatious grin.

The girl stood on her tiptoes and jumped for the book. "You have no right to take it!"

"Settle down. You're lucky I'm showing you any attention." Still holding the book out of reach, Gerard puffed out his chest. "You seem to not know who I am."

"Unfortunately, I know exactly who you are." She reached for the book again—unsuccessfully. "The other girls talk about you like you're some kind of god." Her green eyes rolled. "Believe me, you're nothing like the hero in that book."

"Nothing at all? If he's a hero, I don't see how that's possible."

Still holding it high, Gerard paged through the tome in search of a description of her fictional hero. The bar maid jumped for it, but he only laughed. She muttered something under her breath.

After he stopped laughing, he said, "I'll give this back, if you let me know your name."

She lifted her chin in defiance. "It's not important that you know my name."

Anger briefly bubbled up inside Gerard, but he pushed it aside and turned on his charm instead.

"No need to be rude. I was only curious what the story is about."

The girl's eyes narrowed. "Give it back."

Gerard clicked his tongue. "You're a strange girl. Why is this book so important?"

"It's one of my only possessions." She clenched her fists. "Please return it."

He glanced from her hardened face to the book. Battles weren't won this way and besides, it wasn't really a challenge with her petite size. The girl had turned a nearly pleasurable conquest into a pitiful experience. There would be a better way to win her over.

"I only wanted to know why you liked the story." Gerard handed the book back to the odd girl, and she stuffed it into her pocket quickly.

Frustrated that her response wasn't the typical one he had been receiving by every other female, he attempted one more time to win her over. He didn't accept defeat easily.

Gerard waggled his eyebrows. "Afraid I might laugh at naïve romance parts?"

Back in possession of her novel, her confidence returned. She crossed her arms. "I'm not afraid. I doubt you could appreciate a tale like this because the hero isn't arrogant. He doesn't brag about how great he thinks he is. He proves it."

Gerard fisted his hands at her implication that he wasn't courageous. "As long as I'm a customer here, you will treat me with respect."

She huffed.

"Or I'll have you relieved of your duties."

"Customer? Ha!" She straightened her shoulders. "You never pay for any of your drinks. Everyone else is too busy kissing your boots and treating you to free ale."

Adele interrupted, "Gerard, please excuse Bellarose. She's new and doesn't understand her place yet." Adele turned to the girl. "Bella, apologize for your rudeness."

Bellarose tucked a loose strand of her hair behind her ear and glowered at Gerard. "Sorry for my impertinence. I tend to overreact when an imbecile messes with my books."

She spun on her heel and stormed away, leaving Gerard staring after her. The high-spirited Bellarose presented a new challenge. Eligible women—and even some ineligible—doted over him. This one wouldn't have been more than a passing flirtation, but her rejection would ruin his reputation as the gift to all women. His jaw tensed. He'd find a way to seduce her, and then once she gave him her heart, he'd drop her. She deserved it.

His mind whirled. If it was the last thing he did, he'd woo this Bellarose out of her shrew-like behavior. Drawing a deep breath and pasting a smile on his face, Gerard turned to Adele. "What's her story?"

Adele rolled her eyes. "She came from an aristocratic family, but her father lost their fortune. He took his family here to escape his debts."

Parents in debt and a spoiled aristocrat brought low, was it? That certainly would be a ticket to winning the girl's affection. "Where is her father now?"

"Dead."

He raised his eyebrows in mocked shock hoping for Adele to give details.

Adele shrugged. "On the ship voyage, Bellarose's parents caught smallpox and died, leaving her with nothing. She was forced to accept the only job she could get." She motioned, and he leaned down so she could whisper into his ear, "You know Gustave only hires pretty girls because we can get men to buy more ale, but she isn't friendly to anyone."

He straightened, mentally comparing his own background to hers. Other than the debt they didn't have much in common.

"So, she must be used to finer things."

Adele nodded. "Yes, but she's no better than the rest of us, no matter how high and mighty she acts." The bar maid stuck her nose in the air in mockery.

He forced a laugh.

"Gerard," she said earnestly, "you'd be better off if you stayed away from her. People like her are why citizens left France." Then, a saucy smile crept over Adele's face. The sharp smell of her cheap perfume filled Gerard's nose. She squeezed his leg. "You know I'm available after work tonight to do whatever you'd like. I'd be much more fun than that stuffy bookworm."

"That's very generous of you, but to be fair to all the maidens, I can't go off with only one." He patted the nearby seat. "But I'm ready to listen if you want to sit for a while and tell me how handsome I am."

Adele giggled and kissed Gerard's cheek, saying as she moved on to the next patron, "Maybe later. I've got work to do."

Not only had Bellarose smelled like flowers and clean air, but she wasn't predictable like the other maidens. Gerard took a pull from his tankard. He would win that girl over if it was the last thing he did.

Chapter 13

Bellarose

B ella dreaded the sight of that egotistical, arrogant man. Gerard harassed her daily, stating to all the patrons that he could coax her out of her shyness. She didn't avoid him because she was shy. She evaded him because he was a toad.

"Good day, Bellarose. I'd like you to serve me with a smile when you bring me my breakfast." He flashed white teeth. "Your smile is one of your best features." Then he looked her up and down.

Bella rolled her eyes while heading back to the kitchen to put in Gerard's order. Quinn happened to be there eating his own breakfast.

He dropped his fork and gulped. "Bella, I'm happy to see you."

"Quinn, I never get to see you in here. I suppose I don't normally fetch the toad's, I mean Gerard's breakfast."

Quinn's eyebrows knit together in question. "Toad? Is Gerard mistreating you?"

Bella didn't want to get Quinn involved because over the weeks, he'd become her protector whenever she ventured outside the tavern.

"Don't worry, I can handle him." She waved in dismissal.

Quinn looked around for his father who didn't approve of him being seen or heard by customers. The cook was busy with his back to the table.

In a quiet voice, he asked, "When will you be able to train some more?" He rotated his wrist in a sword wielding motion.

"Your father has me working until the last customer leaves. Since I'm less... friendly, I do most of the manual work. I can't get customers to buy a lot of drinks like the other girls can."

Quinn frowned, but looked down at his plate when the cook addressed Bella.

"Here's Gerard's food."

She hurried to retrieve it, and Quinn glanced up briefly. He smiled shyly, and Bella felt better knowing she had one friend in New Orleans, but that's all he would be to her. Bella couldn't allow herself to fall in love.

As she delivered Gerard his food, she ignored his attention and tried to look busy sweeping and wiping off tables. She reflected on her life in these mindless tasks.

The happily-ever-afters in fairy tales weren't really how life worked. Her own parents were a perfect example. They may have loved each other truly once, but after they were forced to leave France like common criminals, her parents fought constantly. Her mother spewed hateful words for ruining their extravagant life in France. Bella's father blamed everyone for their woes instead of admitting that his addiction to gambling had ruined them. It hadn't been the corrupt aristocrats that caused him to lose their fortune. He'd done it himself. And dying of smallpox wasn't a romantically blissful conclusion for any life.

Life as a servant was certainly far from her aristocratic life of parties. Her past belonged to one of the characters in her storybooks. She shook her head.

On top of that, Bella would rather be unmarried forever than make a fool of herself like the other barmaids did around Gerard. The pompous war hero was too wrapped up in his own importance to love anyone but himself.

Bella wasn't a fool. She knew he would eventually lose interest in her as he soaked up the attention—attention he didn't deserve—from other females.

"Bellarose," he bellowed, breaking her out of one unpleasant thought into the equally unpleasant present, "get me another cider."

She filled a mug with the fermented drink. Its tangy odor tickled her nose, but she suppressed a sneeze. Though she hated his especially boorish moods, she needed the job.

She turned, mug in hand, and a rush of anger had her tightening her grip on the handle. Gerard had propped his feet onto the table she'd wiped clean only seconds ago.

The urge to push his feet off the surface to teach him some manners almost won, but the tavern owner had threatened to fire her if she continued to be short-tempered with his favorite patron. Gerard brought in the most customers and was excused from normal propriety.

She wouldn't survive if she was tossed out onto the street to beg, but her patience was wearing thin.

As Bella plunked down the mug, Gerard grabbed her arm. "Bellarose, sit down and have a cider with me."

"I'm quite busy." She tried to pull away, but his solid grip on her arm tightened. "I don't think I could."

Adele brushed past and whispered, "Don't be rude."

"Nonsense, I'm like a king around this tavern." He pulled harder. "I think Gustave will allow you to take a break for me."

Gustave nodded to her that it would be all right. The other bar maids eyed her with envy. They'd been nasty lately. Since Bella had caught his eye, Gerard had been ignoring the other girls and refusing service from all but Bella, no matter how much others flirted with him. Adele threw her another dirty look.

Bella's breath hitched, but she sat in the chair beside him, desperate to keep her job and to escape his grip.

Gerard smiled approvingly. "Bellarose is such a long name. Is there a shorter version I could call you?"

"Fine. You may call me Bella." She raised her chin. There was no reason to tell him that she no longer felt like the girl with the extravagant name.

"Well, Bella, I know you're shy, but I promise you that I'm harmless." He winked.

"You don't have to avoid me like I'm some kind of wolf."

You want to bet?

Instead of fighting Gerard, which only emboldened him more, she tried another tactic.

"I'm not afraid of you, but I'm also a lowly barmaid who doesn't deserve attention from someone as famous and heroic as you." Bella scooted her chair farther away and hugged her arms to her body. "I'm not fit to be anyone's wife."

"Believe me, I don't want a wife." Gerard chuckled. "I only want to have a little fun, and you seem to be in need of some entertainment."

Her cheeks warmed. *Entertainment?* She bit her lip, then blew the hair off her face. "I'm happy with my books. I don't deserve any more than that."

"No one deserves my attention, but I'm such a generous fellow that I give it out graciously anyway." He pulled his shoulders back and made his muscles bulge through his shirt.

Bella couldn't believe his obtuse conceit. "Seriously?"

"When it comes to talking about myself, I'm always serious." Gerard grabbed Bella from her chair and pulled her effortlessly onto his lap. "Isn't this more comfortable?"

Bella clenched her fists. Worries about losing her job were replaced with fury. She jumped off Gerard's lap and slapped his cheek with all her strength.

"How dare you!" Bella's voice cut through the other bar noises. "You self-centered swine!"

Gerard rubbed his cheek, and his expression turned deadly. "You wretch! You could have had a pleasant time. I'll make you pay for this."

He stood up. "Gustave! Come here! Immediately!"

The Swan's owner trotted out of the kitchen, mopping his sweaty brow with a handkerchief.

"What is it, Gerard? Do you need more ale?" He paused and looked nervously between Gerard and Bella, his gaze settling on the red mark on the soldier's face.

"No, he doesn't need more ale. He needs to keep his hands to himself." Bella put her shaking hands on her hips. "He forced me to sit on his lap!"

"Hush, Bella. Let Gerard speak!"

Gerard scowled. "Being under the impression that Bella desired my attention, I gave her what she wanted. Then she slapped me hard across the face." Gerard rubbed the red welt. "I mistook her insults as flirting, but her physical abuse is the last straw." He stood to his full height and glared down at Bella and Gustave. "She needs to go, or I will never come back to this establishment!"

"Gustave," Bella protested, "I never encouraged nor flirted with—"

"Bella, you no longer work here!" Gustave's loud interruption showed no interest in her point of view. "Take your few belongings and leave! No one is allowed to treat this fine young hero like that." He turned to her and narrowed his eyes, adding in an undertone, "And I can't afford to lose his patronage."

"But—he—"

The tavern owner pointed at the door. "Don't say another word. I give you a job and a roof over your head, and this is how you thank me? Leave, Bella!"

Gerard's self-righteous smirk mocked Bella as she scurried to the room she shared with Adele. Fighting tears, Bella hurriedly tossed her cloak around her shoulders, grabbed her belongings—one other simple dress, a thin nightgown, and two books wrapped in felted wool—bundled them in an old sheet that she tied to a stick to make carrying it easier.

Where would she go? For a moment, she thought about Quinn, her only friend. He'd wonder where she went. However, not only did she not want to risk any more humiliation, but if Gustave caught her searching for his son, she wouldn't be the only one to suffer. Gustave lashed out at Quinn enough already. She would have to be content with the memory of his warm chocolate eyes and the way his smile lightened her moods. These would be a constant companion to salve her wounded spirit.

Still, her heart ached. Leaving without saying goodbye might be the best thing for both of them, but perhaps she could send word to him once she found a new place to live.

Bella avoided the taproom, where the other barmaids were lavishing attention on that self-important bully and kissing his reddened cheek. Not wanting the brute's attention, she edged behind a group of men and slipped out the kitchen door.

The sun should have been out, but instead unusual weather forced rain drops to pelt her tear-stained face, adding to her misery. Bella slouched and held her arms near her body as she sloshed through the wet streets. While Gerard was worshiped for his rotten behavior, she was forced onto the road—soaked through, homeless, and disgraced.

She closed her eyes for a moment. No house, no money, no friends, except for the son of the man who'd thrown her out.

Her misfortunes seemed to swallow the present as she plodded over the cobbled streets—rain and misery her only companions. Despite the bone-cold damp air, she didn't regret slapping Gerard. Her lips pinched at the thought. He'd taken liberties he shouldn't have. The Swan wasn't a reputable place, but that didn't mean she was without morals. He was the worst man she had ever met and deserved the worst fate life could give him.

Again, Quinn entered her thoughts. She quickly shook off the notion that he could be more than a friend. Just because she thought about him a lot, it didn't mean she loved... Anyway, if he had been allowed in the tavern, he would have stood up for Bella's honor. Why, the night before, he'd scared off the drunken sailors who approached her in the alley. Bella was meeting Quinn for a sword fighting lesson when the men blocked her way. Quinn thrust his sword toward them and with clever foot work and swipes, he managed to pop the buttons off their shirts and trousers. They ran holding their falling pants.

Her steps slowed, and she dodged under a low hanging eave. Bella hadn't met many obnoxious men before coming to America. While he was still alive, her father had kept them away from her, and after her parents had been buried at sea, the sailors called her unlucky and avoided her. She'd learned how to avoid the ship's crew and keep to herself.

Thankfully, when she arrived in Louisiana, Quinn had been near the ship's docks. He had rescued her from unsavory men that day too. If Quinn could have stopped Gerard, maybe she'd still have her job.

Bella sighed. Life wasn't fair, but why couldn't things go well this once?

She was thankful for her work shoes. Adele had given her the pair because they fit Bella's smaller feet better. The footwear was more suitable to her current circumstances than the ones she wore from France. Adele noticed Bella's blistered feet one evening in their room when she attempted to wrap them in rags. It was true Adele was hard on Bella, and jealous over Gerard's attention, but she had initially attempted to help Bella navigate her new job and life. Bella's mind drifted toward bitterness as her stomach growled, but she ruthlessly pulled it back. What else could she be thankful for?

Bella trudged down empty streets. The deluge of rain probably forced everyone inside. Normally the homeless hung out in the alleys, but even they must have found shelter. It was as if the whole world had turned its back on her. She dashed water from her face and kept going. She needed lodging and work, but not a soul—

"Young lady!"

Bella spun around. An ancient woman crouched in an alley.

"Why are you out in the rain? You'll catch your death." The woman's voice shook, but her brown eyes gleamed like a twenty-year-old's.

"I have nowhere to go." Bella drew close. If she was cold, how much colder would an old woman be? It only took a second for her to decide. She pulled off her wool cape, the one luxury she hadn't sold upon reaching New Orleans. "You shouldn't be in the damp weather either. Here take this. It didn't get too wet."

The woman shook her head. "Don't worry about me. I'm hardy and healthy as a horse." She pushed the cloak back to Bella. "Besides, I have a home to protect me from the elements. I'm not a beggar. I needed some fresh, wet air." Then she chuckled. "I think you need my help. I know you need a job and home."

Bella's eyes widened. "Yes, but how—"

"You said you had no place to go, and that means you can't have any money. So, either you don't have a job, or your employer is a louse for not paying you." The woman clapped her hands together. "I know the perfect solution to your dilemma."

Skeptical curiosity prompted Bella to say, "I'm listening."

At once, the rain stopped, the clouds broke apart, and vanished. *Almost like magic.*

"Go up the hill in the north part of town." The old woman pointed a crooked finger up the street, and a clean spicy scent wafted from her clothes.

"You will find a lovely plantation that no longer has servants. The plantation belongs to the Count and Countess de la Rose."

Bella gasped. "My family knew the de la Roses when they lived in France."

"Then surely they will welcome you into their home."

"Perhaps." Bella narrowed her eyes. "How do you know so much about their affairs?"

The woman smiled mischievously. "You would be surprised by what I know."

With that, the stranger vanished as if she had never been there. Bella blinked and rubbed her eyes. She knew that the woman couldn't have disappeared—like magic—yet a sulfur odor replaced the spicy one.

Bella shook her head. "She probably lives close-by and ducked into her house." Then she whispered, "Magic only exists in books."

She didn't know a lot about plantation life, but it had taken a myriad of servants to keep her family's French chatêau running smoothly.

Asking for a job from the de la Roses would be mortifying. Her father had told her they were the richest and most cruel family in France.

"I can do this."

Bella straightened her back and walked toward the estate with self-assured steps of what hopefully was her road to salvation.

Chapter 14

Gerard

Even though the barmaids kissed the red spot Bella's slap left, Gerard fumed. That impetuous girl had dishonored him. For a few seconds, Gerard felt a slight twinge of guilt that Bella had been forced to leave her job, almost as if Elayne were at his side, once again shooting down his pride. Bitter sorrow welled up again. Elayne was gone. The flicker of remorse disappeared.

His foul mood grew, and Gerard shrugged off the pretty young women who doted on him. Maybe it was time to leave The Swan and find a real job. Praise over his exaggerated deeds no longer filled the void Elayne left.

The war was over.

At that moment, he didn't care if he was honored or spat upon. Even so, he didn't leave, just downed his cider. Eventually, the fawning women left and he stared into his cup.

"Are you Lieutenant Gerard of King Louis's army?"

Gerard's head came up.

A short, stout gentleman in a white-wig, a fine waistcoat, and matching breeches peered up at him. Gerard frowned. Even damp from the storm outside, someone of this man's caliber was still too fine for the lower-classed tavern.

"Yes," Gerard said. "You may call me Gerard."

The man slightly bowed. "I have an important message to give you from General de la Rose."

Gerard swallowed the last of the cider to drown the memory of the day he lost everything. "He died in the war."

"I know, but he kept me on retainer in France to find you and give you a message for him in case he and his wife died." The man pulled out a silk handkerchief with the letters *C.A.* embroidered in red thread.

He wiped his brow. "The General didn't know you would be living in America, or he would have found a lawyer to deal with this matter in Louisiana." The man eyed the patrons who had been staring at them in interest. "Is there somewhere more private where we may talk?"

Gerard harumphed. "You came all the way from France to give me a message?"

"It's a little more complicated than that." The man leaned in and whispered, "I'm here to see that his estate is taken care of and deeded over to his next of kin."

"I'm confused." Gerard's brows knitted together. "What does this have to do with me? You should be speaking to his relatives."

"If we could speak privately, I will clear up all your confusion. Your involvement in these matters is imperative."

"Fine, as long as you keep it short. I have things to do." Gerard stood, taking satisfaction that he towered over the fine gentleman. "We can go to my room upstairs and talk."

The man bowed again. "I'm sorry if this seems an inconvenience, sir, but I promise you, it will be worth your time."

"Follow me." Gerard stomped past the bar and climbed the steps to his lodgings.

The man followed behind Gerard to the quaint room that contained a small table, chairs, and a narrow bed.

Gerard motioned for the stranger to sit across from him at the table, then grimaced. The man smelled of sweat, fancy cologne, and wet wool. He wiped his face again with the handkerchief and set a satchel on top of the table.

"General de la Rose left you something in his will." He said quickly as he pulled documents out of his bag. "I asked to speak to you in private because I didn't want any unsavory people to know your business."

"Don't worry about the patrons of The Swan. They may seem a little suspicious, but most of them are decent folks looking for a little distraction from their everyday lives." Gerard eyed the documents. Then he bragged, "My presence scares off the true criminals. There were rumors that pirates used to visit The Swan, but they didn't want to mess with a war hero, so they go to other pubs."

"Yes, I've heard of your battlefield exploits." The man nodded. "However, I'm not here about that. I'm here to settle the de la Rose family estate business. I believe you will be quite pleased over what Count Garren has deeded over to you."

"I forgot he was a Count—wait!" Gerard's brow wrinkled. "Deeded over to me?"

"Exactly. The General had more money than he could have spent in a lifetime. His wife passed away a few years ago, so his sons automatically were next in line to inherit his wealth. But I'm getting ahead of myself. First, let me introduce myself to you." He held out his hand. "My name is Charles Alexandre."

Gerard shook his hand, then scanned the papers on the table.

"This is from Count Garren." Monsieur Alexandre handed a waxed-sealed letter to Gerard. "I will let you read it first before I say any more."

Gerard read the note, disbelief growing by the second. He devoured each line, anger and sadness rolling like cannon fire on a battlefield. Then he read it again. He sat, silent, staring at the strange words. Before he spoke, the memory of General de la Rose's letter handed to him on the battlefield minutes before the general died. Surely, it wasn't addressed to him? Had he even read the name and address on the communication?

Without explanation, Gerard rushed to where he had stashed the note. He grabbed it, and the seal on the dispatch broke open, almost as if he'd broken it himself, even though he hadn't—*magic*?

He started reading as he crossed the room to the table.

Dear Gerard,

I am your father. This letter will explain why you didn't—you couldn't—know until after my death.

A powerful enchantress visited us during your fourth birthday festival. She accused your mother and I of selfishness and took you away to live with a farm family.

The enchantress wanted to teach us a lesson by erasing you from everyone's memory except for your mother and mine so we could regret our actions daily. This has always been a matter of unending grief for her and myself.

I wished I could have told you how proud I was as I saw you bravely fight our enemy, but as I already explained, that was impossible.

Your mother has already passed, but once I die, I will be able to tell you via letter. I want to bequeath your inheritance to be shared between you and Antoine, your brother.

The enchantress threatened us with worse repercussions if we didn't change our ways, so we moved to America to escape her magic. Your mother and I have always loved you, but saw her capabilities firsthand and believed her words if we disobeyed them.

All my love,

Father

Count de la Rose

Gerard set the letter down and looked at Monsieur Alexander. The lawyer smiled, but Gerard felt as if his chair had been pulled out from under him.

Chapter 15

Bellarose

Each labored step worsened Bella's glum mood. Since it was after noon, the sun was at its hottest. The rain and heat created a dank humid atmosphere. Bella's muscles ached pulling each step from the thick, deep mud. Sweat trickled down her back. Bella inhaled the smell of fresh mowed hay from the nearby field that blended nicely with the rich soil scents. It was an improvement from the tavern's mixture of tangy spirits and sweaty men.

Bella sighed in relief when she finally neared her destination. The white stoned home stood tall with multiple stories, towers, and turrets. It wasn't a typical Louisiana mansion, but rather, it resembled her home in France, the château that Count de la Rose had sold to her family—the place her father gambled away. Discouragement pulled her further into depression, not only at the reminder, but also at her current state.

She bit her bottom lip. Once they saw her dismal appearance, they'd refuse to give her a job. Then what would she do?

There was nowhere to clean her mud-encased shoes, and the hem of her dress was thoroughly soiled. Even though she had another dress in her bundle, she couldn't change, and these were her only pair of shoes. She stepped onto the plush lawns to wipe them on the grass, but they were stained.

"I hope no one looks out the window to see me," she mumbled, casting upward glances.

Once she'd scraped most of the muck from her shoes, she straightened, jutted out her chin, and approached the large doors. Intricate carved gold roses were attached to the wood on the entrance, further reminding her of her old home in France.

She knocked twice. No one answered. She banged a little harder, and the enormous door squeaked open.

Bella peeked inside. "Hello? Count de la Rose? Countess? Is anyone home?"

Her voice echoed, but a tittering was the only response. When no one appeared, she pushed open the door and squinted in. The only illumination came from the sunlight beaming through the high windows. Cobwebs encased the gold sconces and chandelier above the entry way, and dust motes danced in the beams of light.

She stepped in completely.

The door shut behind her.

Bella jumped and spun around, but she was alone.

At least it was daytime. The thought of being alone in the cobweb festooned house made her shudder.

Bella's eyes adjusted to the darker interior, and she scanned the grand entrance before moving any farther. It *was* a duplicate of her previous home.

"Is anyone here?" She called.

Only her echo came back to her.

"Maybe," she whispered, "they're away for a retreat. Maybe they took their house-staff with them." She stepped past the grand staircase, determined to find the servants quarters. After all, no one was there to tell her she wasn't hired. She might as well start working. The entire place was a mess.

The rooms were exactly like the château in France, making it easy to find the empty quarters. Before her family's flight from France, Bella didn't have the first idea how to tidy a house, but months at the tavern taught her the basics. Gustave assigned her the task of mopping floors and other cleaning duties when she was too haughty with patrons. He might have meant it as punishment, but she was thankful for the work. If she was cleaning, she couldn't be expected to flirt as the other barmaids did to sell extra cider. She straightened her shoulders at the thought. Though no longer the proper French aristocrat, she wasn't loose with her morals.

Once she'd changed into her dry clothes, she set to work.

It was odd the de la Rose family had left the house abandoned long enough to gather dust. Even when Papa had fled France, he had left servants behind, though he hadn't paid them. A pang of remorse hit her, but she brushed it away. It hadn't been her fault.

But here, if she could prove her worth, perhaps when they returned home, they would gratefully hire her. In the meantime, she had a roof over her head. Surely there was something left in the kitchen, so she could probably find something to eat. The Swan's cook had taught her how to make some simple dishes. She wouldn't starve.

Once the entryway's cobwebs were vanquished, she stopped to catch her breath.

"Perhaps that old woman knew more than I originally thought." Bella blew a loose strand of hair away from her face. "Though, how she knew doesn't matter."

She was no longer homeless, for which she was thankful but she would eventually have to face the de la Roses, and their reputation for cruelty didn't give her a lot of hope. She would cross that bridge when necessary. For now, she needed to accomplish as much as she could before the sun set, then she would give herself permission to eat. The large pendulum clock on the table inside the parlor indicated that it was already two o'clock. In the fall, the amount of daylight was shorter.

Bella found cleaning therapeutic. Rowdy customers no longer interrupted her, leaving her free to ponder the last few months' events. From a luxurious home much like this one to the belly of the ship, to the paltry quarters she'd shared with Adele, where her only escape was *The Scorned Fae.*

"If I was as rich as the de la Roses, I would pay someone to read books to me while I cleaned." She chuckled. "Although if I were that wealthy, I wouldn't be cleaning. I'd read the books myself."

She wiped her hands on the white apron she found in the kitchen. Her knees and back ached after scrubbing the floors of several rooms. Despite the pain, scrubbing old dirt was better than clearing tables at The Swan where vile men ogled her or made lude comments.

A sudden scuffling noise startled her. She sprang to her feet.

"Is somebody there?"

The odd sound immediately stopped, but Bella's voice repeated back at her from the vaulted ceiling. Mice, maybe? She shuddered. The home had been vacant long enough for rodents to be sharing the space.

Bella scrunched her nose, then said loudly, "I hope the family and servants return soon, but if I have to, mice, I will be the one to exterminate you."

She lifted the heavy bucket of water, but when she glanced back into the room she'd just cleaned, a thin layer of dust covered the floor she'd mopped. The bucket dropped to the floor splashing dirty water over her shoes.

"This is futile!" She blew a loose hair off her face. "How is everything I've already cleaned dirty again? If I didn't know better, one might think magic was afoot."

Her words resonated back, and the hair on her arms rose. Bella shook her head, refusing to allow the ridiculous notion a place in her mind. It was only that her imagination was cultivated by fairy tales she'd read as a child. With a sigh, Bella prepared to clean the hallway floor again, a clomping noise came from a nearby bedroom. She jerked her head toward the sound, her heart pounding.

"Is somebody in here?" She tiptoed to the door, and her hands shook slightly while she scanned the space. She took a deep breath. Hadn't that furniture been in a different spot?

A high-backed mahogany chair stood in the middle of the room where no furniture had been before. Bella had dusted every surface in that area before scrubbing the hallway floors. She could have sworn the chair sat in the corner.

"Curious," she whispered.

She moved the seat back into the corner, but a loud banging came from the front of the house. Someone was at the door.

Chapter 16

Gerard

Gerard showed Monsieur Alexandre the note General de la Rose had given him.

"I was with the General when he took his last breath. He handed the letter to me, but I forgot. Someone I loved died next to him." Gerard's throat tightened, but he held the two letters side by side, scanning them both.

"How is this almost identical to the one you gave me? How is this even possible?"

Monsieur Alexandre dabbed at his moist forehead with a mono-grammed cloth and stammered, "I-I- assure you, this is not a hoax. Being under strict instructions from the Count, I didn't read the letter, but he told me in essence what it said." He composed himself and folded his hands. "He paid me a great amount to follow his instructions after his death. I'm only doing what I was paid to do. The rest will be up to you. The plantation your father left you isn't too far from here, but he said you will have to share it with your brother."

"This can't be true." He paused to gather his thoughts, but his words came out harsh. "My parents died when I was four. I only have adopted siblings—no blood relatives."

"Your father didn't tell me the circumstances or why you were sent to live with that poor family, but then that is none of my business."

The lawyer pointed to the clean letter. "Count Garren vowed it's all in that note."

Wordless, Gerard rubbed his chin and stared at the letters.

Monsieur Alexandre pulled out a longer document with the Count's formal signature at the bottom. "If you would sign here"—Monsieur Alexandre pointed to the line next to the Count's signature—"then my job is complete."

"What's this?"

"It's the deed stating that you inherit half of your father's estate. You also inherit half of his wealth. The rest, of course, goes to your brother as he told you."

Gerard stared in disbelief at the legal document.

The lawyer crossed his arms. "I haven't had any luck contacting your brother. No one comes to the door when I knock. Perhaps you can explain to him how important it is to sign his part of the documents?"

"Monsieur Alexandre," Gerard asked, "was the count—was my—father mentally stable?"

"Your father had a sound mind. Insanity didn't run in his family."

Gerard nodded absentmindedly, more preoccupied with the ludicrous story his "father" had written in both letters. An enchantress sounded like nonsense. Hidden heirs? Ridiculous. And yet, with a simple signature, he would be a wealthy man.

He signed the paper.

"Very good," the lawyer grunted as he gathered his belongings.

Charles Alexandre paused at Gerard's door. "You need not stay at this *inn* any longer. Collect your possessions. My carriage waits out front, and I will take you to your new home before returning to my hotel. Until my ship leaves, I'm staying at the Royal Sonesta hotel."

Gerard had paid in advance and owed no allegiance to The Swan, so he said, "Thank you," as he made quick work of packing his few effects. Everything he owned fit into a sack. He followed Monsieur Alexandre to his fancy carriage, which tipped when Gerard stepped into it. The lawyer huffed, told him to move to the middle to balance his weight, then climbed to sit next to the driver, muttering all the while.

Gerard didn't look back as they left the tavern. Instead, he focused ahead on his too-good-to-be true adventure, The carriage bounced down the cobbled streets and onto a dirt road. While the rain left behind a clean, earthy aroma, the roads were a muddy mess but the enormous black Clydesdales pulled the laden carriage through the muck.

Curiosity beat out skepticism. Gerard fixed his eyes on the countryside, where a large white castle-like building loomed among trees and fields.

As Monsieur Alexandre's carriage climbed the hill that led to the de la Rose plantation. Gerard's thoughts turned, oddly enough, to the young bar-maid Gustave had dismissed because of his insistence. For a second, a flash of guilt hit him, that he was moving up in the world—if the lawyer wasn't lying—while his comments had driven a young woman to the streets.

That ill-tempered shrew didn't deserve a second thought. She deserved to lose her job at the tavern. She'd been daft for turning down his advances.

Again, he imagined he heard Elayne's musical voice. She wouldn't have liked his recent behavior.

But Elayne was dead.

He pushed that smidgen of regret aside. Instead, a different and unexpected anxiety took hold. He owned a plantation. He had a brother.

If the supposed enchantress had erased Gerard's existence from everyone's mind of when she stole him away from the family, his brother Antoine didn't know about him either. Fleeing to escape the enchantress seemed ridiculous to Gerard. If magic truly existed, wouldn't the enchantress be able to find them anywhere in the world?

The carriage brought them down a driveway that was lined with towering trees that led to a gravel courtyard. It stopped in front of the opulent white stone home. Off to the sides of the ornate door were tall arched windows and turrets which reminded Gerard of a French château he saw once when he was a child.

This was his. He cared about his family in France, but a snake of envy ran through him. How very different his life would have been if he'd grown up here.

The carriage shook as Gerard stepped down. He stood tall, thinking how his six-feet-five-inches and broad muscular body was proof that he was worthy of this mansion. This was a hero's house, and he deserved it.

Monsieur Alexandre interrupted Gerard's thoughts. "Make sure you ask Antoine to come and see me as soon as possible. I will be leaving on the next ship sailing to France."

Gerard nodded.

The lawyer laboriously climbed down from the driver's seat, hoisted his body inside the carriage with a grunt, then signaled the driver with a knock. The coachman clicked his tongue and jiggled the reins. The horses walked around the circular entrance and picked up their pace down the long tree-lined driveway. Gerard watched the carriage disappear below the hill before he moved.

He pivoted toward the large gold-embellished doors. It was now partially Gerard's home, but he thought it was best to announce his arrival. When no one came after the first gentle tap, Gerard banged louder the second and third time. Still, no one answered. Gerard frowned. Monsieur Alexandre had said he couldn't contact Antoine. Maybe Antoine no longer lived here?

Before he could knock again, the door creaked ajar. Gerard squinted into the empty hallway. Certainly, a place so massive needed many to maintain it, but no servants greeted him. The natural light that filtered through dirty windows was dim as twilight approached, and no candles brightened the dim interior. Would servants leave the place in such a state?

"Is anyone here?"

His deep bass voice boomed and echoed back at him.

A scuffling noise accompanied the reverberation, but it didn't sound human. He scowled. Hopefully, the place wasn't infested with rats.

"Hello?" He spoke louder. "My name is Gerard, and I own half of this—"

"What are you doing here?"

Gerard's eyes widened as he turned to face the small woman wearing a dirty apron. "I could ask the same of you. You're the last person I expected to see here."

Chapter 17

Bellarose

Hoping someone from the de la Rose estate would greet her, Bella hurried to the entryway. Instead, the booming voice of that odious man from The Swan rang through the halls. She'd recognize that arrogant tone anywhere.

"What are you doing here?" She held up a candelabra to get a better look.

"I could ask the same of you. You're the last person I expected to see here."

Bella lifted her chin defiantly, "I work here, and *you* are trespassing."

"I have paperwork to prove the contrary." He pulled out the deed from the inner pocket of his jacket, then paused. "You work here? Since when? And, what exactly is your job?"

Bella wiped her hands on the apron. "Could you please leave so I can continue my work?"

"No. I own this place, but I'm a gracious man." He bowed slightly. "I'm willing to forgive your rudeness and the horrible way you treated me at The Swan if you'll answer my questions."

If he truly owned the place, she would have nowhere to go.

Bella clenched her fists. "You arrogant boor! I don't have to do anything you tell me to do!"

Gerard flashed Bella a large, white, toothy grin and jiggled his eyebrows up and down in a flirtatious way.

"I'm the master of this estate, and you will be wise to treat me as such." He slightly paused. "You may call me, Master Gerard."

Bella paled. Had he been telling the truth when he claimed the house as his?

"I thought... What do you mean?"

Gerard smirked. He pulled out the legal document and pointed to his signature. "I inherited half of this plantation. Evidently Count de la Rose was my father."

Bella gasped. If that was the case, she had lost again, but she wouldn't let him see her cry. She blinked away her tears, turned, and climbed the grand staircase in front of the entrance.

"Wait!" Gerard yelled. "You can't walk away from me. I command you to come back."

Bella pivoted to glare at him.

"I will be looking for another job in the morning!" She couldn't keep the sarcasm out of her voice, no matter how she tried. "You will never have control over me... Master Gerard."

Bella twisted, hiked up her skirt, and continued her ascent up the stairs.

She reached the second story when Gerard asked, "Do you have a place to live?"

"No," she replied. "But the street is a more pleasant home than one with an egotistical toad."

"Bella, wait! I think we could both benefit from this unplanned arrangement."

She spun around and glared at him.

"I can't care for this place by myself, and I don't think you will survive long on the streets."

He was right, though she didn't like admitting it.

For a moment, his arrogant expression faltered. "I don't know where the servants are and I need you to help." Gerard cleared his throat and drew a breath. His conceited sneer was back on his face. "I can forgive your disrespectful behavior because I'm in a charitable mood. And it's quite clear that you need my help."

Bella stomped her foot, and the lie tumbled out, "I don't need anyone!"

Gerard gave an affected sigh. "I know my charms are too much for you, my dear Bella, but where will you—"

"I am *not* 'your dear' anything!"

"Get food and a place to sleep?" he continued as if she hadn't protested. Gerard smiled smugly. "If you help take care of this place, I'll allow you to live here without strings attached. I doubt you will find a better offer in town."

"You are the most infuriating man I've ever met!" she spat back at him.

"Calm yourself and come back down here so we can talk in normal tones."

She paused several minutes while weighing her options. Finally, she descended to the second step to stay close to his eye level. "I am calm, and I will remain that way, if you leave me alone."

Gerard backed away slightly. "Does that mean you will stay?"

After several seconds she replied, "I will if you promise to leave me alone."

"I agree to your terms, but you may get lonely in this gigantic place." He winked. "And I'm a great companion."

"I will never be lonely enough to want your presence." Bella stepped away from Gerard. "I'm not a barmaid who will flirt with you, nor will I boost your overinflated ego. I want to be treated with respect. Do I make myself clear?"

Gerard crossed his arms over his massive chest. "Have it your way, but you'll regret it. Most females find my company a treat. You can live here in exchange for cleaning this place and cooking. I won't talk to you unless it is related to your employment."

"Thank you." Relief flooded her. She curtsied and even offered a half smile.

Gerard watched her through narrowed eyes, and her smile vanished. He glanced past her into the gathering shadows.

"Now that we have that settled, I need to find Antoine, my *brother*. Was anyone here when you arrived?"

Bella shook her head. "I haven't come across anyone."

Gerard frowned. "I knocked first, and the door opened on its own."

She licked her lips. "Yes. The same thing happened to me. When I saw the dust and cobwebs, I wondered if the residents were on a holiday of some kind. I began cleaning to impress the count and countess, but it doesn't seem I have accomplished much."

Suddenly strange whispering interrupted the temporary break in conversation.

Gerard jerked toward the sound. "Is anyone there?"

"I think we're hearing rats—or ghosts." Bella scanned the room. "I've been hearing those noises all day."

"Ghosts?" Gerard's eyes widened.

Bella grinned. "I'm jesting. I don't believe in ghosts."

Gerard shot a glare at her "Don't you find it strange that this place is empty?"

"Yes, but as I said, maybe they left town for a holiday."

"Monsieur Alexandre, the Count's lawyer, believes that my brother, Antoine still lives here. Maybe he left after the Count died."

Bella gasped. "The Count is dead?"

"Yes, along with his wife." Gerard sounded matter-of-fact. Didn't he have any feelings for the de la Roses? They were his family.

"My mère told me of the grand parties they attended at the Count's home in France before we moved to America. I'm sorry about their deaths." Bella sighed. "When the old lady in the village told me they needed servants, I thought that perhaps they could give me employment as a favor to my deceased parents."

"What old lady?"

Bella averted her eyes. "I don't know. She came out in the rain, but disappeared before I learned her name."

"That's odd, but then, today is full of peculiar happenings." Gerard held up the deed to the mansion. "Until today, I didn't know the de la Roses were my parents. I was raised by a poor family near the count's estate in France."

Bella gaped at him, momentary sympathy displacing her dislike for the man.

"All I have to explain my current situation are two unbelievable letters from Count de la Rose. It is too absurd to believe, and yet, Monsieur Alexandre said the Count's will states that I am their son."

Bella drummed her fingers against the side of her leg. "Are you really the master of this place?"

Gerard nodded. "According to the documents I signed, I own half of this estate, and my brother owns the other half." He looked around, as if his words would bring his sibling. "I thought he'd be here to help straighten out the details."

"How is it possible to not know that the de la Roses were your family?"

"This letter"—Gerard pulled out a wrinkled document from his inner waistcoat pocket—"is far-fetched, but it explains the details of the separation."

Gerard handed her the letter. As she read it, her eyes widened. Why would he trust Bella with this information? Maybe the situation was as surprising for him as it was for her?

"Far-fetched, indeed." Bella returned the paper to him, then twisted a loose hair around her index finger. "The count blamed a magical enchantress on your separation. I've read fairy tales about them, but that's the point—they're fantasy."

"Exactly. Until I speak to Antoine, I'm left with more questions than answers." Gerard tucked the letter back into his jacket. "I was planning on getting things figured out today, and then I could tell my family in France about my good fortune." He exhaled. "Their lives would be so much better if I could share my wealth with them."

Bella almost smiled, but shook her head. "I get the impression from that letter that wealth only made the de la Roses miserable. You were probably better off with a different family." She added quickly, "Although, based on your behavior toward me at The Swan and when you first arrived here, you have perfected the act of a spoiled aristocrat."

Gerard clutched his chest in mock horror. "I don't know what you mean." His expression shifted for a moment into one of... grief? He scrubbed his hand over his face, then asked, "Do you know if there is any food around here? I'm starving."

Bella blinked at the turn in conversation. "That is one of the many peculiar things about this place. The kitchen is full of fresh food. It's as if the family and servants aren't really gone." She pointed to the chandelier above their heads. "But the cobwebs tell a different story."

"Since there is food, can you cook?"

"I can cook something simple after I clean up. I didn't work at The Swan long, but I did learn a few domestic skills."

Gerard's smug look returned, and he rubbed his stomach. "Then me getting you fired was meant to be, because I'm starving and no one here but you know how to cook."

Bella sighed heavily. "You're too much." Then, she climbed the stairs and left the mansion's new owner alone with the cobwebs.

Chapter 18

Gerard

While he waited for Bella to fix dinner, Gerard ambled around the grand mansion in search for clues to the whereabouts of his brother. Late afternoon sunlight fell through a door ahead of him, so he followed it into a study. Huge paintings of the French country-side and portraits hung on each of the walls. A gold-framed painting of a young General de la Rose and a beautiful fair-haired woman hung above the fireplace. Was she the general's wife—Gerard's mother?

He felt temporarily sad that he didn't remember the countess. He compared her to the mom whose round face always had a smile for him. Countess de la Rose looked stern. His mother's once black hair turned salt-and-pepper in recent years and Gerard supposed he would take after her rather than his balding father, but then he always had to remind himself that they weren't his real parents. Yet, staring at the countess's fair hair, he saw no resemblance. Gerard briefly smiled over the memory of how even though he towered over his adopted mother, he still felt like the small boy whose tears she wiped whenever he got hurt or was sad. A burst of resentment for the lies he believed about his family lingered.

If anything in the letter was true, he'd inherited his thick, dark hair from his father. But the more he examined the portrait, the more he could see similarities between the general and his own appearance, but the count had russet eyes. The countess had the same vivid blue color as Gerard's. The bar wenches always complimented the color to feed his ego.

"They're a handsome couple."—Gerard puffed out his chest—"a trait I obviously inherited."

With a single glance back at his handsome parents, Gerard left to explore the other rooms on the ground floor. His growling stomach reminded him he hadn't eaten since breakfast. Finding the kitchen was his first priority. Bellarose—no Bella—she had told Gerard the shortened name was all right for him to say. Anyway, she better have the meal ready.

The sun sank, dimming what light fell through the windows, but his thoughts kept returning to the letters' claim and the proof hanging in that study.

Before the war, he had occasionally wondered about his real parents, but now he couldn't stop thinking about them. What kind of life would he have had if he hadn't been taken—or given—away? Also, why hadn't he ever seen them since they lived so close to the farm home where he was raised in France? Had they simply given him away and lied to everyone, then run for shame?

Gerard raked his fingers through his hair.

Why hadn't the enchantress allowed General de la Rose to tell Gerard he was his father before his death? It seemed cruel of the enchantress—if she was real. He snorted. It was more likely that the Count had lost his mind and imagined Gerard was his son than his parents had let him live with a poor family his whole life.

After all, what kind of parents would allow that to happen?

His jaw clenched. When movement caught his eye, he spun to confront it, but it was only a mirror. He glared at his reflection in the dirty glass. The strong-jawed man who looked back was already a hero.

He would have loved to share this mansion with Elayne, but no—she's dead! He temporarily wished this was one huge mistake no matter how rich it made him.

He turned away from the mirror. He still half-heartedly hoped to gain Bella's admiration. After all, he was handsome and now rich. She wouldn't find another man as great as him in this empty mansion. She wasn't Elayne, but a little female attention would help keep his nightmares at bay. Gerard didn't like solitude. Lonely silence brought too many memories. Bella could be the interruption he needed.

The sun edged toward the horizon, and the mansion grew too dark for a stranger to navigate. The flickering candles, he assumed Bella had lit barely lightened the gloom. Still, they were better than nothing. Gerard grabbed a golden candelabra. An unfamiliar female voice cried, "Ouch!"

The hairs on the back of his neck raised. Maybe there were ghosts instead of rats?

"Who's there?" He squinted into the darkened spaces around him. Facing enemy fire was one thing. Facing the dead who were unwilling to move into eternity was entirely different. How was he supposed to deal with specters?

He tried to sound commanding. "I demand you show yourself."

"Since you're holding me, it's difficult to reveal myself."

Startled, Gerard released the candelabra.

It dropped, the flame extinguished before the metal hit the floor. A face appeared, trapped behind the gold plating. Gerard's breath hitched, and he edged back as the candleholder slowly straightened itself upright.

"You have a firm grip, sir." The golden face scowled at him. The candles relit, and the young maiden's voice continued, "Just because I'm a candelabra doesn't mean I don't have feelings. That hurt. Now,

I wouldn't have said anything, but I was not expecting such a strong grasp."

"I- I- must be hungrier than I thought." Gerard blinked, then shook his head. "I'm hallucinating."

Inanimate objects that spoke? Gerard left the candles and fled the scene fumbling through the darkening hallways.

A dim light glowed not too far ahead, so he moved cautiously toward it, avoiding objects—and candelabras—along the way. The light grew brighter the closer he got, and to his relief, the kitchen greeted him, bathed in the glow of firelight. Flames from the hearth heated the space while Bella chopped vegetables on a large wooden island in the middle of the room. She scraped the vegetables into a black pot hanging over the fire, and then looked up at him.

"Good. You found me. I need your help." Bella wiped her brow with the back of her hand. "Make yourself useful and go outside to fetch me some more wood."

She pointed to a door near the hearth.

His fear at the encounter with the candelabra vanished. Gerard folded his arms and glowered down at the insolent young woman. "Did you forget something?"

Bella's brow scrunched. "No. What would I have forgotten?"

"I'm the master, and *you're* the servant." Gerard flashed a toothy grin. He wasn't afraid of work—he'd grown up on a farm, after all—but he *owned* this mansion now.

Bella's emerald eyes narrowed, reminding him of the stray cat who hung out at his home in France. The cat hadn't been a friendly feline, but she'd kept the mice away. His mouth twitched. This young woman's prickly personality mirrored the cat's snarly one in every way.

"Master Gerard, would you be so kind as to fetch me some firewood so there will be enough to cook your food?" She curtsied in an overly dramatic way and went back to stirring. "I would do it myself, but I thought you wanted to eat. I'm preparing stew as quickly as possible."

Half offended and half impressed by her sharp tongue, Gerard almost held his ground. He might not have had his own servants before, but he had observed Gustave at The Swan and the tavern owner hadn't put up with attitudes. But before he answered sharply, his stomach grumbled.

She lifted a brow, and he stomped outside.

A little voice whispered that his rudeness had forced her sour behavior to rear its ugly head, but he pushed the thought aside. No, he'd win her over eventually. After all, he was—what had the patrons in The Swan taken to calling him? Gerard the Great. Bella would get over whatever was nagging at her, and realize she was lucky to have him as the master of this estate.

The autumn sunlight fell over the small yard with its stacks of wood. Despite the day's rain, Louisiana's oppressive humidity had dropped, making the air cooler than it had been. The outdoor temperatures, however, lacked the crispness of autumn in France. He missed the snow and rain.

The moist air strengthened the scent of cut pine from the wood pile, but the softer fragrance of sweet roses mingled with the smell of freshly cut wood. Gerard couldn't see where it was coming from, but even with the setting sun he saw well enough to chop wood for cooking and heating their rooms in case the evening cooled.

Gerard took off his jacket, then his waist coat. His biceps stretched as he swung the ax. Again, and again the sound of metal on wood sliced through the quiet landscape. Sweat trickled down the middle of his back, but he enjoyed the exertion of physical labor, even if it would cause sore muscles in the morning.

He thought about the hours he spent at The Swan sitting compared to the hours he spent plowing fields or feeding the livestock in France. He realized he had become a little lazy after the war.

Once the pile was satisfactory, Gerard hefted a sizeable amount of kindling, but a deep growl startled him. He spun to face the noise. Some of the wood fell as he scanned the land behind him. It sounded like a wild animal.

The beast was probably looking for an easy meal, so Gerard made a mental note to locate weapons. No predators would harm him or Bella. He rolled his shoulders and strode toward the kitchen, though he listened, ready to turn and fight. He'd taken down a bear before. Whatever this beast was, it wouldn't have a chance.

He backed into the kitchen without dropping the wood. "Here's fuel for cooking. I cut enough to heat our rooms too, but I left the rest outside. I'll grab more after we eat."

Bella nodded without looking up. "Where is your room?"

"I haven't chosen one yet." When he neared the pot, delectable aromas of cooked meat and vegetables made his mouth water. "That smells delicious."

Bella's cheeks pinkened. "Thank you."

Gerard stepped out to gather the clothing he had left next to the wood pile. No sign of any animal. Pulling on his waist coat, he stepped back inside.

She stopped stirring, turned, and smiled. "I know the perfect place for you to sleep."

"Where?"

Bella smirked. "Back in France—oh my, did I say that out loud?"

Despite his growling stomach and the sweat on his brow, Gerard flashed her a grin. "You're lucky I have a good nature. Don't forget who the master is and who's the servant. *You* are a penniless girl, and you need me, whether you want to admit it or not." His grin widened. "Besides, I'm nice to look at."

She grunted but didn't frown like before. Perhaps he was making headway.

Bella spun around and shoved two bowls and two mugs into Gerard's chest. "Here make yourself useful."

"What do you want me to do with these?"

"Put them on the table, and here." She put two spoons into the empty bowls. "We'll need these also. I'll bring the stew."

"Isn't setting the table your job?" Gerard caught himself before admitting he had done it many times in his farm home. Bella didn't have to know that.

She clenched her fists. "The more you help me, the sooner we can eat."

His stomach rumbled again "Where's the table?"

"You really are a pain in my side." She grabbed some towels and wrapped them around the pot handle to lift it from the fire. "Follow me."

Bella led Gerard to the dining room, but before they reached the table, large clanging noises erupted from the kitchen. She gasped, and the stew pot slipped. Gerard let the bowls fall to the ground and snatched the pot's handle.

"What in the world is that?" Bella's face had gone pale.

Worry shot through him. Had he shut the door? What if that wild animal got brave enough to come inside? He squared his shoulders. "Let's find out."

Chapter 19

Bellarose

B ella sidestepped the broken pottery and moved closer to Gerard's side. Together, they cautiously approached the kitchen.

"Let me go first in case it's someone or something dangerous."

Bella glanced at his hands. "Are you going to scald it to death with stew?"

Gerard glowered at her, before setting the pot onto the hard wooden floor. He scanned the hall, but when his gaze settled on the candle holders nearby, he shuddered.

It didn't make her feel any better that the giant of a man was apparently afraid of a candelabra.

"I won't need a weapon. I can fight with my fists." Gerard lifted his clenched hands to flex his muscles.

If Bella hadn't been frightened by the sounds from the kitchen, she would have rolled her eyes.

Gerard cautiously opened the squeaking door. Then he pushed it wide open.

Both he and Bella stood there, gaping at the kitchen staff bustling around the large room. Some servants were cutting meat and vegetables, and one put another pan into the brick oven.

A pretty dark-brown-haired young woman rushed forward. "*Bonjour. Je m'appelle* Brooke," she said in clumsy French. "Oh, I hope you know English."

Before either Gerard or Bella could ask any more questions, the sound of Brooke's shoes clicked away from them.

"Something rather strange is happening here." Gerard rubbed his chin.

"I know." Bella frowned. "We weren't imagining anything because of hunger."

"Also," Gerard demanded with a growl, "where's my brother? He's supposed to be living here too."

Gerard sat down roughly onto a red velvet armchair. Bella joined him onto the nearby identical one. She wanted answers, and hoped Brooke would return soon so that she could ask them. A porcelain figurine of a fairy was on the polished table between them. The face looked oddly familiar to Bella, but her thoughts were interrupted when the mantle clock chimed seven times and the sound of shoes clicking proceeded.

Brooke announced, "Dinner is served."

Bella followed after the beautiful young woman. Gerard didn't offer her his arm, of course. Brooke led them into a large banquet hall where a table that could have seated sixteen sat in the center of the room. Three gold-rimmed dinner plates with matching golden flatware were grouped at one end of the table. Steaming dishes of roasts, and vegetables surrounded Bella's stew. To the side, smaller plates held rolls of freshly baked bread. Bella's knees actually weakened at the welcome sight. Brooke left, but Bella suspected Gerard hadn't noticed. The food had his full attention.

Gerard licked his lips. "Everything smells delicious."

"How did they get it ready so—"

"Good evening."

Bella spun to face the door.

A finely dressed young man in tan breeches, a white ruffled edged shirt, and an azure vest that brought out the color of his eyes entered. Bella noted that he didn't wear a wig as his shoulder-length blonde hair hung loosely. He offered slight bows to them both.

"My apologies that I wasn't here to greet you earlier, but I was enjoying some recreational hunting in the nearby forest. I'm Antoine de la Rose."

"But that would mean..." Bella's whisper faltered. She glanced at Gerard, who had gone pale. Was this truly the burly young man's brother?

"I'm sorry, but I don't know either of your names." Antoine continued, "I was already running late and didn't stay to hear everything Mademoiselle Brooke tried to say."

"I'm Gerard." He flushed, then blurted, "How old are you?"

"An odd introduction." Antoine lifted a brow. "Eighteen."

"I-I'm your brother." Gerard's cheeks reddened, then he stood even taller than usual. "I'm eighteen. We must be twins even though we look nothing alike."

Bella quietly inhaled as she glanced at both men who were attractive in their own way. Antoine was slightly shorter, but almost as broad shouldered as Gerard.

Gerard motioned toward the door. "I saw a painting of our parents. I definitely take after the count, and you the countess."

Antoine's gaze skimmed over Gerard. "I see your resemblance to Father, but how do you know we're brothers?"

"I received this letter today."

Gerard pulled a document from his inner pocket and gave it to Antoine, who read with intensity. Bella watched them both, mentally comparing the two men. Antoine's clothes were precise, but he looked exhausted—as if he were ill. Gerard, on the other hand, was the perfect picture of strength and muscle, even if his clothes were more worn and his hair untidy. Antoine was beyond wealthy. He needed nothing. Maybe that hunting excursion had been too much for him—or maybe it was something about living in a house where dust traded places with sparkling cleanliness.

"This is my father's handwriting." Antoine's hand shook slightly. He set the letter on the long table and pressed his hand to his side. "Where did you get this letter?"

"That one was given to me this afternoon by a lawyer named Charles Alexandre. He had been retained by Count de la Rose. Monsieur Alexandre tried to explain what happened to our parents, but he didn't give me a lot of information."

Gerard pulled out a second, brown stained letter and set it by the first missive. "Your—I mean *our*—father handed this to me on the battlefield."

Was that... blood? Bella shuddered.

While Antoine studied both, Gerard raked his fingers through his hair. "Monsieur Alexandre has been trying to meet you to finalize the will and ownership of this estate. He wants you to come to his hotel in New Orleans and sign some documents." Gerard paused and fidgeted with his sleeve. Bella assumed he was giving his brother time to take in the implausible account, which stirred up a story she read about a cursed plantations or she *was* reading it—she shook the strange thought out of her head before it took root. She already had too much to handle and didn't need to add farfetched thoughts to it.

Antoine raised startlingly blue eyes to level a stare at Gerard, who shrugged and said, "I'm still trying to wrap my head around this information since it seems too unbelievable, but we equally own half of this mansion and half of our parent's wealth."

"Father told me about his will before he went to war, but he said I wouldn't be able to know who the other joint-owner of this estate would be until after he died." Antoine frowned and broke eye contact. "Based on this letter, the enchantress didn't want me to know about my own brother until my parents' death."

Gerard shifted his weight. "Until today, I didn't know anything about my real parents or this mansion. The family who raised me told me the old lady who gave me to them said my parents died." He collected the letters and tucked them away. "I'm still somewhat skeptical—of that story about an enchantress."

Bella wondered if she would rather have Gerard's situation with parents who died with secrets or parents who died with their public shame. He still had an adopted family, but if she were in his situation, she may be slightly resentful. Either way, they both understood loss.

"I've witnessed magic this past year," Antoine said abruptly, his expression shifting to something wild and unfocused. "I tend to believe what Father wrote." He moved his shaking hands to his side. "I will straighten out matters with Monsieur Alexandre, but I'm rarely home. Could you bring the lawyer here one evening for me to sign the documents?"

And people accused Bella of being entitled? She might not like Gerard much, but indignation made her ask, "Why don't you do that yourself? Gerard is your brother, not your servant."

Antoine gave an awkward laugh. "Never mind, I'll ask Brooke to arrange it. You don't need to be bothered. Very well, I accept that you're my brother, but it will take a while to get used to the fact that I'm not an only child." His smile returned, and he walked over to Bella. "Now, for a more pleasant topic, who is this vibrant young lady?"

Bella curtsied and forced a smile onto her face, as her mother had taught her, even though she wasn't sure about either young man. "My name is Bellarose Bonnay, but you may call me Bella. My parents were the Baron and Baroness of Bourbon. They came to your parents' parties on several occasions when they lived in France."

"Then we are almost friends already." Antoine gently lifted her hand and pressed a kiss on her knuckle. "So, how did you end up in my home without your parents?"

"It's a long story, but your brother is partially to blame." She wished her eyes could cast daggers at Gerard as she glowered at him.

"Gaging by that glare you gave Gerard, I bet it's an interesting story." Antoine chuckled. "Let's discuss it over food. Dinner has waited long enough, and I'm ravenous. What about you two?"

Chapter 20

Gerard

T he conversation was stilted while they ate, but Gerard didn't care. He focused on eating the best food he'd tasted in his entire life. Bella primly cut her food into tiny pieces, and Antoine lounged in his chair at the head of the table. The small annoyance that Gerard felt at Bella being at the table instead of in the kitchen with the rest of the servants vanished as he had second and third helpings of the venison and potatoes.

The scents of savory meat and warm bread made it difficult for Gerard to slow his pace. Bella took dainty bites, but her eyes darted back and forth between him and Antoine. She reminded him of a curious—or maybe nervous—cat. He attempted to chew with his mouth closed as Antoine and Bella did, but neither he nor his brothers took time for manners on the farm. The habit of eating quickly to beat your siblings to the last helping of bread had been a game. Also, he was forced to shorter meals during war time, which required taking large bites and quickly chewing. He gave up trying when the buttery potatoes hit his mouth. It didn't matter anyway. He half-owned this plantation.

Servants efficiently kept the elegant crystal goblets filled with a bitter wine. Gerard missed the simple taste of ale or cider from the tavern. He hesitated before he grabbed the last buttered roll, but a cook brought out another full basket immediately. Antoine eyed Gerard as he scooped another helping of vegetables onto his plate and Gerard couldn't decipher if he was being judged harshly or examined for better understanding. Resentment for Antoine's privileged life stirred inside and blended with a desire for his brother's approval, which only added to Gerard's already convoluted emotions.

The clatter of silverware against fine China seemed exaggerated and as Gerard's appetite was satiated, he began to notice the lack of conversation.

Antoine sipped his drink, then set it down precisely on the table. He finally broke the silence. "Bella, how did you end up at Rose Manor?" He turned toward Gerard before she answered. "That's what my parents called it. Mother insisted on a rose garden here that surpassed the rosarium we had in France. But I digress. What brought, the lovely Bella here?"

"I needed a job thanks to your brother." Bella shot eye-daggers at Gerard.

His jaw tightened. "You lost your employment all on your own."

Bella's attack on his honor was unjust. Not only was she a pauper, but Antoine hadn't witnessed her impertinence to see that Gerard was justified in his behavior. Gerard also felt that because he generously allowed her to stay at his house, she needed to let go of what happened. Why did she have to continue holding a grudge when it was Bella who acted atrociously to him?

Bella huffed. "That's a fib, and you know it." She turned back to Antoine. "An old woman told me this estate lost its servants. When I showed up, the place was vacant, so I decided to stay and clean." Bella stared intensely at Antoine when she asked, "How did all your servants arrive here as if from thin-air?"

"Strange," Antoine said as he moved food around the plate with a fork. For a moment, Gerard thought his brother was going to explain, but no, Antoine was focused on Bella. "You claimed your family knew mine. Isn't your family affluent? Why do you need to work or find a place to live?"

"I..." Bella blushed. "My parents died on the journey from France."

"They were running from debt collectors." Gerard added.

Bella's glare burned holes like hot coals and his own temper rose to match it.

"Ah. And you had to earn a living when you arrived." Antoine took another slow sip, then asked, "Why did you lose your job?"

Before Bella blamed him for anything, Gerard said, "No matter what she says, it wasn't my fault."

"Oh wasn't it?" she fumed. "That is not—"

"Bella was a bar maid. A rude bar maid, who is basically a criminal." A rush of self-satisfaction at her indignant gasp overtook his anger. He said smugly, "Not only is she running away from debt collectors, but she entered Rose Manor without invitation and made herself at home."

Bella's face contorted in hostile rage despite the slightly sagged shoulders, but then she slapped her hand on the table. "Let's set this straight! You wanted my help when you thought this place was empty. I was doing you the favor!"

Antoine's sudden laughter interrupted the argument. "You two will make this place much more entertaining. You fight like brother and sister."

Gerard and Bella exchanged hostile glances, then directed those looks at their host. Antoine continued to chuckle. A stout woman with brown hair pushed a dessert tray laden with strawberry tarts into the room. Even though he'd already gorged himself, Gerard's mouth watered.

"Thank you, Mrs. Watson," Antoine said casually.

She curtsied and left, closing the doors behind her.

Antoine eyed the dessert. "We have a greenhouse to grow the berries out of season."

While Gerard reached for a pastry, Bella said, "Antoine, where did she come from?"

"The kitchen," he replied. "Try one of these tarts, before my brother eats them all."

Gerard had already scooped up every last one onto his plate.

She scowled. "Thanks for leaving some for me."

He washed down a bite with a whole cup of tea. "You might dress like a pauper, but you act like a rich girl, putting on airs."

She gaped at him.

Antoine leaned back against his chair and regarded Gerard closely. "Your manners are wanting, brother."

Gerard narrowed his eyes. "Unlikely."

"Your behavior is atrocious." Bella flung the words at him.

"My behavior is perfect for a war hero and your master." Gerard smoothed his shirt. "Show some respect."

"It is you who should show respect to the lady," Antoine said.

For a second, Gerard felt the weight of Elayne's disappointment. Had he treated Bella poorly? Before the thought took hold, he pushed it away and popped a strawberry tart into his mouth.

"Do you have anything to say, then? Or were you thinking conceited thoughts about yourself?" Bella asked.

He swallowed the pastry. "Is there ever an end to your foul behavior?"

"Foul? That's the pot calling the kettle black," Bella chided.

"Brother, you bring out such pleasantness from dear mademoiselle. I must learn your charms." Antoine wiped his face with the cloth napkin. "This must be your upbringing."

"Fine." Gerard stiffened, then pushed the plate to Bella, who snatched up one pastry. "There is no reason to insult the people who adopted me."

Antoine rubbed his chin thoughtfully. "This interaction triggered a memory. I recollect knowing a boy about my age. Mère didn't want me to talk about that boy—probably because he was you. Now it makes sense. According to Père's letter, I wasn't supposed to remember that I had a brother."

Gerard took another bite of the tart and spoke in between chews. "I know you think Father's letter was truthful, but it seems a little far-fetched, don't you think?"

"What other explanation do you have for ending up with that farm family?" Antoine placed a finger against his chin. "How is it that you had no recollection of me or our parents until now?"

"I was young. Maybe that lady kidnapped me, and left me at the farm for fear of the consequences." Gerard put his fork down. "What I can't understand is why our father didn't say anything to me when I was a soldier in his unit—not even while he died on the battlefield."

Antoine's eyes became glossy. "Earlier, you said you talked to him before he died?"

Gerard nodded. "I was in his unit."

"The letters clearly state that the enchantress forbade him to tell you the truth until he and Mother were dead." Antoine stared past the table, and a far-off expression washed over his face. "I envy you for being able to see father before his last breath."

"It sounds like you miss him," Bella softly said. "And it sounds like you believe in magic."

He nodded.

"Does…" She bit her lips, then pressed on. "Does that explain why this mansion was vacant and dirty only an hour ago, and now it is a regal, well-cared-for estate?"

Antoine's blank-stare vanished into a smile. "Brother, I would like to get to know you better and find out what's happened to you since you left me. However, I have had a long day and must retire to my quarters. I'm leaving early in the morning, but I will see you both at tomorrow night's dinner."

"Where are you going? I could join you," Gerard offered.

"No, I'm afraid that my business is of a personal nature."

"You're not going to answer any of my questions?" Bella asked.

"My dear, I don't know what you mean." His smile seemed more forced. "I'm sure Brooke will help you with any assistance you need."

"She isn't much help either," Bella mumbled.

Gerard blinked at her. She attempted to stand but wobbled on her feet and sat again.

Antoine stood quickly.

The taste of the delicious strawberry dessert lingered on Gerard's tongue. Brooke entered and began clearing the dishes.

The day had been bizarre and taxing. Bella, too, must've felt the weight of it, for she slumped forward. Before her head hit her empty tart plate, Brooke moved the dish to the side, as if she had known Bella was going to drop.

Strange.

Gerard's eyes drooped threatening to close without his consent. He leaned forward. Brooke hurried to his side and removed his dessert plate. His head dipped, and he managed to set his arms on the table before his head hit the fine linen.

As Gerard drifted into oblivion, he heard his brother say, "That was close."

Chapter 21

Antoine

Once Gerard's head hit his arms, Antoine finally relaxed. "There for a while, I wasn't sure if he'd leave any of the tarts for Bella."

Brooke bent to check the girl's breathing. "She's fine. I was unsure how much of the slumber potion to add, but as deeply as they're breathing, they should sleep until morning."

"We'll have to get them to bed, though." Antoine hesitated, then touched his brother's broad shoulder. "Stay with Bella. I'll carry her to the Rose Room in the east wing after Pierre and I drag Gerard to..."

"To his bedroom," Brooke finished for him. "The room your mother had prepared for him."

"I never knew."

"You couldn't," she said softly.

"Gerard is the reason she set aside that one bedroom." He deeply frowned as he glanced between Bella and Gerard's still bodies. "How long do you think we will be able to keep our secret from them?"

Antoine felt a mixture of elation, fear, and torture. He trusted Brooke's wisdom. He admired many things about her especially how calm she was under stress.

Brooke exhaled loudly. "I think we should tell them the truth."

"Won't that only create more problems?" Antoine rubbed his neck.

"But Aerowyn said if someone did something unselfish for you out of love, the curse would be broken," Brooke protested. "One of these two may be our saviors."

"I doubt my selfish brother or this girl will be the spell-breakers. Besides, I'm only able to talk to them for a few hours at night, and I really don't want to involve them in my mess."

Antoine lifted Bella just as Pierre appeared in the doorway, as precise as always.

"I'll drop off Bella and be right back to help move Gerard before I get out of these clothes."

The Rose Room wasn't too far. He shifted Bella in his arms as he gently placed the unconscious girl onto the bed.

He pulled off her shoes, draped a soft blanket over her, and smiled wearily. "I hope you find this to your liking."

Suddenly a growl escaped from his throat, and he checked the clock on the mantel. How had time gone that quickly?

He dashed back to the dining room, where Pierre, Brooke, and two footmen had wrangled Gerard onto a sling. Antoine led the way back to the bedroom next to his—the one he'd seen only a handful of times. Pierre fumbled with a key, and the door swung open.

Antoine paused at the threshold. Mère had forbidden him to enter this room. Once, soon after they arrived in Louisiana he had peered in when the maids entered to clean it, and the toys captured his attention. Fantastic, wonderful toys. But, Mère had caught him spying and quickly shut the door.

"You must forget what you saw in there," she'd told him.

For weeks, he had prowled the hall, trying the doorknob in disobedience, but it was never unlocked, and eventually, he had almost lost interest.

This evening, he finally understood why, and he and his currently human servants were carrying a sibling he never knew existed into the forbidden room. Toys still lined one wall, but he barely noticed them as they hefted Gerard onto the bed.

The servants bowed and left, Brooke pausing to set a gentle hand on his arm.

He was alone with his brother.

Strange, but nothing seemed impossible to him now. After he was cursed, magic was no longer only in fairy tales. Things he had valued before weren't important to him anymore because Aerowyn's spell had changed his priorities forever.

Before the hex, the world owed him everything. His status as an aristocrat gave him the right to take whatever he wanted from whomever. Though his parents had tried half-heartedly to teach him humility, they weren't much better when they justified using slaves to work.

At the time, it seemed perfectly acceptable to treat other so inhumanly, but Antoine finally realized how atrocious his parents really were for owning slaves. Of course, they attempted kindness, bestowing gifts of toys on the less fortunate, but no gifts could make up for the cruelty of treating humans as property.

The Count and Countess had given Antoine whatever he asked—except what was in this room. Maybe they'd forgotten Aerowyn's warning, or perhaps they were making up for the empty void left by Gerard's absence when they overindulged Antoine.

It didn't matter now. They were dead, and Antoine was afflicted with Aerowyn's final judgment for his appalling, self-centered behavior. He wrestled between love and disdain for his parents when he recalled their flaws.

The longer he experienced the cure's effects, the more hopeless he grew. For a moment having his brother back gave him a new optimism, but then he chided himself for expecting things to improve. Whenever he anticipated something positive, he only opened his heart to agony and disappointment.

Another growl escaped. The wild thing that threatened to control him was emerging. He ran down the stairs toward the back door before it was too late.

It wasn't even midnight yet. The transformation was occurring earlier than it ever had before. As the enchantress's deadline approached, he spent less time as a human. Aerowyn had warned Antoine that if no one showed him unselfish love by his nineteenth birthday, he'd be hexed forever—a beast without a human conscience, and his birthday was next month.

Until then, Antoine had memories of what he did when he was the beast. Sometimes the man in him sought human companionship, but the wolf won over and wandered back into the forest. It was for the best that the wolf didn't linger because the animal's dangerous instincts could threaten people it faced. In wolf form, he was unpredictable though his human side wrestled for control. Antoine was exhausted from the two natures battling for dominance. He was resigned to let the beast take over in the end.

He dashed around the woodpile and haphazardly discarded his clothes. He needed to be far from Gerard and Bella before he completely transformed. His skin prickled, and he headed for the trees.

Sharp pain immediately tore through tendons and bones. A shriek muted the ripping skin, and soon, the scream disappeared into a disoriented whine and pant. The beast had a brief instance of human understanding before it loped into the nearby forest.

Chapter 22

Bellarose

B ella opened her bleary eyes and winced at the pain pounding in her temples. Despite the headache, she was comfortable. She stretched. Yes, the plush mattress was similar to the one from her previous life—so different from the bed she used at The Swan.

The realization forced her upright. She rubbed her eyes. A white canopy fringed with intricate lace stretched overhead, and the coverlet she lay on was embroidered with red roses. The fabric was as luxurious as her bed in France, and it smelled as if the flowers were real.

"Where am I?" She whispered to the empty room with its walls covered with rose patterns and gold embellishments.

The memory hit. *Rose Manor!*

Last night she had eaten dinner with Antoine and Gerard, and she had been tasting that delicious strawberry tart, but then her vision had blurred. Had she fallen asleep at the table? She had no recollection of walking to this room, and surely, she wouldn't have fallen asleep in her clothes and stockings.

Someone must have placed her in bed after her embarrassing behavior. Gerard? Or Antoine? Her cheeks warmed at the thought of the handsome Antoine carrying her here.

She studied the room. It was the size of her bedroom in France. Homesickness hit. Even though going from an aristocrat to a pauper had bruised her pride, it had been worse to experience an overwhelming loneliness that stifled her hope of happiness. She felt alone among people like she was isolated in a proverbial tower. She had nothing in common with anyone in Louisiana, but Quinn, and she didn't know when she would ever see him again.

For a second last night when Antoine had arrived, she had felt a small optimism of returning to her former status, but the truth was that she would have to work for everything she received from now on. She wouldn't take anything for granted ever again.

Two familiar books on the nightstand caught her eye. She reached for them and realized they were hers. In fact, all of Bella's sparse belongings had been moved from the servant's room to this one. Her drabby work dress, a drastic contrast to the room, was draped over a chair sitting in front of a vanity dresser.

Who had brought her things to this room? Brooke? Surely not Gerard?

A small amount of sun peeped through the cracked drapes. She scrambled out of bed and shoved her feet into her bedside shoes. She stopped at her reflection in the mirror. Bella couldn't clearly see her face, but she imagined fear and grief created dark circles and worry lines. She walked to the windows and opened the curtains to allow full light to wash over the room.

For a moment, she stood transfixed by the Louisiana autumn. No clouds blocked the blue sky, but signs of the season were present as tree foliage had mingled colors of orange, yellow, and green still lingering from the summer. This was her first October away from home. She leaned her forehead against the window. Louisiana falls weren't the same as those back home.

From her vantage point, Bella could see both the flower garden and the wild, wooded area that bordered it. Colorful roses filled the area, and for the briefest of moments, she thought she smelled them, even through the window.

Suddenly, a brown and white wolf appeared under the pines. She gasped. It stared back at her with human-like blue eyes. The creature was beautiful, but Bella shuddered. It wouldn't be safe to go outside with such a ferocious beast wandering. Just as suddenly as it had appeared, the wolf vanished into the forest, but her concern didn't. What if that wolf had attacked her while she walked to the mansion the previous day?

She forced herself to turn back to the window and gasped again. The whole room had changed. It looked like it hadn't been cleaned in months.

Just like the other parts of the house had looked before all the servants materialized out of thin air.

Ever since she arrived at the mansion, nothing was ordinary—but then again, what was ordinary? Her life had taken so many turns that she no longer had any expectations for it.

She crossed to the armoire and searched for her other dress. It hung in the very back on a lavish gold hook. She couldn't help but notice the expensive gowns hanging next to hers. The fine fabrics and styles were assuredly designed for an aristocrat.

A pink taffeta gown caught her attention. She didn't take it out, but she stepped in front of the standing mirror, held up her brown hair, and pulled out small ringlets while imagining how the dress would look.

Her eyes closed as she envisioned a dashing young man bowing low to request a dance. He would wrap her in his arms while music played. She took a few steps, then hummed and swayed around the room, pretending she was in the arms of a prince from one of her books.

Before Bella got too far into her daydream, however, a feminine giggle made her jump. Bella immediately stopped twirling. It had been too high pitched to be Brooke or Mrs. Watson, but the bedroom door was still closed. She shivered.

"Who giggled?" Bella addressed the air.

"No one."

"I heard you!" Bella spun around. "Come out, please."

"I can't," said the same girl.

"Where are you?" Bella's voice quivered as she peered behind the furniture and knelt to look under the bed.

"Here."

The voice came from above Bella's head and chills ran down her spine.

"Where is here?" Bella stood.

"I'm not allowed to tell you."

Bella stopped, and put her hands on her hips. "Why aren't you allowed to tell?"

"Because," she answered.

"Are you spying on me?" Bella's hands shook. She wanted to sprint away, but was temporarily paralyzed.

"I'm not spying! And it's not your room. It was the Countess de la Rose's guest room." The girl finished in a whisper, "But she died."

Bella stepped back and followed the direction of the voice. The canopy frame above the bed posters had a decorative round piece surrounded in rose embellishments, and inside the circle was a face of a little girl. Bella blinked and rubbed her eyes in disbelief. The girl smiled back at her. Bella's arm-hairs stood straight up, and she ran.

Once down the stairs and several hallways away from the possessed furniture, Bella slowed. Maybe it was only her imagination going wild again. Until the tarts, she'd felt perfectly fine. Maybe her sudden sleepiness caused an illness that made her see things. That was the most logical explanation. Slowly, her breathing calmed.

Even though it was daylight outside, the hallways were dark. No natural light illuminated the corridor. Bella looked for a candle or lamp without success, so she found her bearings and set on a mission to find Brooke or Mrs. Watson.

She was determined to get to the bottom of this mystery, no matter what she had to do. And if she wasn't to be homeless, she needed a job, haunted mansion or not.

Chapter 23

Gerard

*E*layne stood in the middle of a battlefield, blood seeping through her dress. Gerard ran to save her, but she was encircled by the redcoats he had massacred out of anger for her death.

She called, "Help me!"

His throat tightened in a sharp scream that pierced the air, but the dead British soldiers with oozing head wounds and slashed throats somehow tripped him and swore at him for ending their lives. The coppery smell of blood churned his stomach as the dead men grasped and pulled at Gerard's legs. He couldn't reach her. He was trapped in the midst of death and devastation.

Then, Elayne morphed into a different woman, one who had the same golden hair as Elayne but her eyes were violet instead of blue. No gentleness shone from her eyes or face. She wore the same gold pendant around her neck, and it glowed in the sunlight.

"Look at what you've done," she cried. "You are as beastly as the rest of your family. You will pay dearly for your evils!"

"Who are you?"

She did not respond.

He couldn't free his feet and legs. The bodies held him in place. He toppled as crimson liquid gushed from each wound pulling him into a sea of blood.

Gerard jerked awake, gasping for breath. His damp hair clung to his neck. As accustomed as he was to nightmares, this one hit him especially hard. Slowly, his heart stopped racing, and his breathing calmed. He wiped his sweaty brow and narrowed his eyes to peer into the dim room.

Something was off about his surroundings. His eyes narrowed into the darkness. A speck of sunlight glimmered through a crack not too far away. Gerard gingerly exited the bed and made his way toward the light. He reached out and pulled the curtain open. He squinted at the blinding sun, his eyes quickly adjusting. Below his window a rose garden stretched across the back of the plantation's grounds. Beyond the maze of bright roses was a forest of pine, hickory, and oak trees.

Though the windows were closed, the aroma of roses filled his room. When he turned to inspect the chamber, Gerard noticed the abundance of toys that filled the space. What might have been memories flashed through his mind. Had he truly pretended the ship that was now sitting on a shelf took him on adventures with his father?

Gerard shook his head. Whether or not he had, he needed to focus. He was sure he'd heard Antoine say the previous night as Gerard passed out, "That was close". What did his brother mean? Brooke and his brother must have put something in the tart to make him and Bella fall asleep, but why?

Well, rather than mulling over his brother's potential motives, Gerard intended to confront Antoine. Gerard pulled on his boots and confidently entered the hallway, though he left the door open to light the dark corridor. All the other rooms were closed off, which made the area hard to navigate.

Gerard looked for a lamp, but only found a fallen golden candelabra on the ground near the bedroom door.

"Not this again," he muttered. "So, do I dare pick you up? Am I going to imagine seeing another face in the gold?"

The candelabra righted itself, and candles lit. A voice similar to Brooke's said, "Pick me up and find out."

Gerard gawped. He kept his eyes on it as he backed away swiftly, and then jogged from the delusion.

The previous night's hallucination might have been caused by hunger, but after that dream... What if ghosts from the war haunted him? Nightmares were bad enough. He loathed when they spilled over into the day.

Panic forced him to run, but Gerard couldn't see where he was going. It wasn't long before he bumped into someone and toppled over the smaller frame.

"Oof!" Bella exclaimed. "What on earth are you doing? Get off of me, you large oaf! I'm suffocating!"

Absolute terror eased into something like amusement. He wouldn't ever tell Bella that she was the distraction he needed to escape past terrors.

"I guess you literally fell for me." Gerard jumped to his feet and offered her a hand. "Is my handsome face more than you can handle?" He winked, though she might not have seen it in the dim hallway.

"You big brute! You ran into me! I was being careful to avoid tripping over anything in the dark. Whyever did you think running in an unfamiliar, dimly lit place was a good idea?"

"I like to live on the edge—take chances and maybe crash into a pretty girl."

Bella laughed. "Surely you weren't running for the sake of running?"

"Of course. I needed the exercise." Gerard smiled.

Bella huffed. "You're incorrigible!"

"Thank you." Gerard bowed.

Bella straightened her skirt and smoothed her hair, then moved to the staircase. Gerard followed. Soft sunlight shone through a domed, stained-glass portion above the stairs and entryway, which made Bella's eyes a vivid, emerald green.

Gerard looked up at the dome. "I wonder what time it is. I think I slept in later than usual."

"It's noon," Bella said. "I have a clock in my room, but I never sleep this late."

"I slept like a rock, but I have a theory about why we didn't wake until now."

"I'm sure you do." Bella rolled her eyes. "Do you have one for what happened to all the servants, too? This place is as abandoned and dirty as it was before dinner last night."

Gerard scanned the area. "I don't know. Has anything abnormal happened to you since yesterday?"

When they reached the bottom of the stairs, Bella kept her gaze on the wall and asked, "What do you mean?"

"Strange, odd, really unusual."

Bella avoided eye contact. "You mean something odder than having this plantation go from cobwebs to sparkling clean within minutes last night?"

Gerard rubbed the back of his neck. "I was referring to seeing or hearing people who aren't really there?"

Bella's eyes darted nervously.

"I'm not sure what you're talking about."

She *had* seen something.

"I think you do know," he said, trying to keep the accusation from his voice, "but you're afraid I'll think you're daft if you tell me."

Bella narrowed her eyes at him. "No, you're the only lunatic."

"Why do you have to be so sharp-tongued?" Gerard's lips turned downward. "I've been every bit the gentleman with you."

Gerard's nightmare made him tone down his haughty behavior. Despite Bella's continued rudeness, was he justified in treating her as a subordinate?

"You think you've treated me with respect? What about our time in the tavern—when you forced me to sit on your lap? I don't like being touched—especially not by you. When you made Gustave kick me out, and I lost the only security I had left?" Bellas' eyes met Gerard's with fire. "That doesn't even include all the times you expected me to dote on you like you were some Greek god of war."

Gerard's conscience niggled at him for causing her to lose her job. Elayne would have wanted Gerard to be kinder to Bella. It was only that his pride over her rejection and continual insolence made it hard for him to be the better man.

"Since we arrived here, I've been more respectful. I'll admit I enjoy irritating you, but you make it too easy. Although," Gerard added begrudgingly, "Antoine charms you with very little effort."

"Antoine didn't brag about himself or make me feel beneath him." She huffed.

Gerard faced her. "If I agree to treat you more as my brother does, will you hold back some of your sharp remarks? I may have acted too rashly when I had Gustave get rid of you, but now we both have a chance at a new beginning."

Bella finally met his eyes. "I'll try to stop spouting all the hateful things I've bottled up since I met you." Then she looked away. "But this isn't as much of a new beginning for me as it is for you."

"Why not? Now, that we know the plantation has servants, you don't have to be one."

"Then what am I? A guest?" Bella bit her bottom lip.

Gerard shrugged. He didn't really think about Bella's fate when he had her thrown onto the street. It wasn't the kind of world a single woman could navigate alone, but he was so caught up in his own emotions that he hadn't considered anyone else's feelings.

Bella's voice quivered. "I'm a stranger to everyone here and I can't pay for any basic needs." She turned her head away and wiped at her eyes.

Gerard didn't know what to say. He swallowed hard. "We should find Antoine... Oh wait, he said he would be out today, but then we should talk to Brooke. Maybe she could find a job for you."

Bella's lips curved slightly, but Gerard thought his words temporarily stopped her from breaking down. He was relieved he didn't have to deal with awkward female emotions.

· · • ⚘ • · ·

Gerard and Bella spent the afternoon navigating the dark corridors, opening all the curtains to let in the natural light. Gerard wasn't afraid, precisely, but sometimes he thought he heard muffled whispers from the walls. Whenever he and Bella neared the sounds, they stopped.

Each room of the mansion had a de la Rose flare to it. All the paintings' frames were engraved with roses, and the banisters had the blooms etched in the wood. Even in the large music room, the instruments and book shelves had the signature flower. He approached one instrument that looked like a box. It's lid, which had a painted rose garden scene, was propped open, revealing strings like a harp. Small black and white rectangles covered the flat surface in front of a chair.

He touched one, and a clear note rang out. "What's this?"

"Harpsichord." Bella said distractedly. She was, evidently, enthralled by the shelves of books.

Gerard chuckled. He'd seen that look on faces of village children, looking longingly at trays of bonbons in New Orleans. Bella loved to read.

"Do you know how to play it?" Gerard plunked a few notes.

Bella grinned at Gerard and finally left the books to sit at the bench facing the harpsichord. His haphazard taps had made a pretty noise, but when Bella began to play, the melody's bright tone made him think of lush green pastures in France. She smiled at him, stood, closed a lid, hiding those rectangles. Afterwards, she returned to inspecting the bookshelves.

Gerard's eyes widened. "When did you learn to play a harpsichord?"

"My lessons started when I was four. My mère wanted me to marry a rich aristocrat, so she made sure I was educated properly." Bella grabbed a book and thumbed through it. "Dukes and counts—all highborn men—want their wives to be versed in music. They only want their wives to be pretty, stay quiet, and entertain guests whenever needed."

Gerard couldn't comprehend only marrying a beautiful, but useless woman. He loved how Elayne was pretty, but served patients in the hospital. "I wouldn't know about any of that since the family I grew up with had all boys. My mother cooked, sewed, gardened, and raised babies. Most poor families I knew had herds of children to help run the farms. The girls probably learned how to care for their younger siblings—the training that they needed to become wives."

"I find it curious." Bella blew a stray hair from her face. "How did you turn out so arrogant with such a humble upbringing?"

Gerard scowled. "You're quick to point out my flaws, but you're not perfect either."

"I never said I was perfect." Bella narrowed her eyes. "It doesn't make sense how you act like you've been rich all your life. Remember, I grew up around aristocrats, so I know how they treated people beneath them." She paused and looked him up and down. "You act like one of them. Maybe it is in your blood, although I'm nothing like my parents, so that doesn't mean everything. Other than the music lessons, I spent more time reading, climbing trees, and being the opposite of what my mother expected me to be."

The idea of a younger version of Bella straddling a tree limb in a fancy dress made him laugh.

"You? Climbed trees?"

"Yes," she said indignantly. "It's not that funny, but is it so hard to believe?"

He forced his expression under control.

She tilted her head to the side.

"Anyway, why aren't you humbler?"

Gerard examined his fingernails pretending he wasn't mulling over his response. He had treated Bella like she was beneath him because he viewed a bar maid as lower class, but why? Afterall, he was a farmer's son. As a soldier, he had to be brave or allow the enemy to win. His victories gave him self-assurance.

"I think you mistake my confidence with arrogance. Besides, how can someone with my muscular build and rugged good-looks not own it wholeheartedly?" Gerard curled his biceps to show them off.

Bella shook her head "There's a difference between confidence and boorishness."

The accusation of boorishness sent a flush of defensiveness through him.

"You act like the world revolves around you," she continued before he could argue. "Was it the war?"

Memories of that morning's awful nightmare brought a sudden chill. "I..."

She gave him a steady stare. "All that praise you received for your supposedly heroic acts didn't do you any good, but perhaps you weren't always such a cad before the war."

Her observation made him uncomfortable.

Gerard raked his fingers through his hair. "I'm no cad," he argued, but with Elayne's accusation ringing in his ears, it felt like a lie.

"Are you hungry? We haven't eaten anything since the tart last night."

She blinked but accepted the change in subject. "Yes, a little. Where's Mrs. Watson or Brooke?" She eyed the hallway and said half-heartedly, "I suppose I could cook you something."

"You don't have to. There is probably something left over from last night." Gerard added, to see her reaction, "I could even eat another tart."

"I can't eat anything that sweet on an empty stomach," Bella answered matter-of-factly, "but maybe there is some cheese or a roll to eat."

"I really hope there is more of that strawberry tart left."

Bella eyed him. "What is it with you and that dessert?"

"Really? You don't remember what happened after we ate it?" Gerard fixed his eyes on her.

"We went to bed; nothing out of the ordinary about that."

He exhaled loudly. "If you're not willing to admit it, I'm going to. After we ate the dessert, you passed out onto the table. I felt drugged, like I couldn't keep my eyes open, but heard Antoine say, 'That was close.' They knew we were going to fall asleep. That's why we slept so late."

"I do remember falling asleep quickly," she said slowly. "Why, though? Why would they drug us?"

Even though he hadn't wanted to admit anything, Gerard's confession rushed out. "And I hear voices coming from inanimate objects."

Her eyes grew, but she turned away. "What do you mean?"

Gerard folded his arms. "I think you know exactly what I mean."

Bella tucked in her bottom lip before answering. "If... if I tell you, you can't use that against me."

"Why would I when I just admitted that it happened to me? In fact, the candelabra I was going to use to navigate the dark hallway talked to me in Brooke's voice this morning. It also spoke to me last night, so I got a little spooked." He paused and then admitted, "That was the real reason I was moving so quickly through the corridors."

"In *Brooke's* voice?"

His cheeks flamed. "There's no reason to make fun," he said when his temper flared.

Before he did something he'd regret, he walked away and headed outside, ignoring her protests that she hadn't been mocking him.

Fuming over Bella's behavior, he roamed the maze of roses, and ended up at the edge of the forest. Floral and pine aromas mixed in the air, but didn't calm his nerves. When a low growl, however, interrupted his angry musings, he stopped in his tracks. Could it be the animal from last night?

It was his duty to keep the plantation safe, so he headed toward the house to find a weapon. He hadn't gone far when the woman from his recent nightmare appeared at the edge of the forest.

Gerard rubbed his eyes, and she was still there—beautiful, but haunting.

"My dear Gerard, I expected more from you."

He knew that musical voice! Images of a ballroom, lit by candles, filled with guests swarmed through his memories. His parent's ballroom in France?

"Yes," she said before he could speak. "I am Aerowyn. I was the one who took you from your parents when you were four. I wanted them to change their ways before you and Antoine turned out as selfish and horrid as they were." Her voice hardened. "My attempts failed."

Gerard clenched his fists. "You have no right to wreck our lives. If you're really the enchantress who kidnapped me, then your actions were worse than any of mine."

She gave him a steely gaze. "Are they truly? What about all those soldiers you killed out of revenge, even after they surrendered? Did none of them have sons? Wives? Parents?" Aerowyn's brown eyes turned violet. "How dare you criticize me! I put Bellarose into your life to give you the opportunity to show kindness, but instead, you harass her. I put Elayne in your life to teach you about love, but instead, you use her death as an excuse to wall up your heart and be cruel to others."

Gerard clenched his jaw, then growled. He wanted to avoid recalling his rage over Elayne's death and how it caused him to react by switching the blame.

"What do you know about love?"

Aerowyn grimaced. "You know nothing about me."

"You use magic to ruin peoples' lives with the excuse that you're teaching them. Who gives you the right to be the morality judge and jury? Are you perfectly selfless? Are you humble and open to love?"

"Be extremely careful not to provoke me." Aerowyn spat back. "I can make your life so horrible that you'd prefer death."

"You already have! If you truly did send—"

The enchantress disappeared, leaving a lingering whiff of sulfur and spice.

Gerard blinked. Had he imagined the whole thing, or had she really been there seconds ago?

He was tired of the terrors his choices during the war visited upon him. That enchantress, if she was real, was only partly right. The men weren't without blame.

Was war fair? Elayne was innocent, and yet the British took her life.

He kicked at a small rock, and it skittered away. His self-control threatened to slip away, but before it did, the growl sounded again.

It was obviously close. Gerard wasn't going to let a threat remain. He may not know how to do much, but he knew how to kill.

He strode into the mansion in search for a rifle. Bella caught up to him.

"There you are!" She peered up at him. "What are you looking for?"

"A musket or a rifle," Gerard said through gritted teeth.

Her eyes grew round. "Why?"

"There's a beast in the forest. I'm going to kill it. It growled at me last night and a few minutes ago." He glowered at her, then continued his search. "I can't let that thing hurt anyone on the plantation."

"Was it the wolf?" she asked. "I saw a beautiful brown and white one when I looked out the bedroom window this morning."

He threw open a door to find a breakfast parlor. He slammed it shut and searched the next room. "I didn't see what growled."

"But there was something different about it, Gerard."

His eyes roamed the next room in search of a weapon. "It is too close to people, and must be looking for food. If it's separated from its pack, it could be starving. I won't let it hurt you or anyone else on my property."

"You can't kill that beautiful creature!"

"Don't be ignorant, Bella. It's not a pet! You're truly the naivest girl I've ever met if you think that wolf won't hurt you the first chance it gets."

Bella darted in front of him and blocked his way. "I know it's not a pet, but it hasn't hurt anyone yet. Please, leave it alone."

"Until you see the horrors this world has to offer, I think you better leave this up to me." Gerard almost groaned with frustration. "I've seen men commit murder without a second look. Why would a wild animal ignore its instincts to survive?"

He disregarded her and continued to search every room until he found a musket hanging above the study's fireplace. He inspected the weapon, and for a second, the scents of gun powder and lead brought memories of the war to the forefront. He shook off the recollections and headed outdoors, Bella on his heels.

He turned to face her. "You should stay inside. If the wolf goes after you, I may not be able to kill it before it hurts you."

"I can protect myself." Bella held up a butcher knife. When his eyebrows rose, she added, "I grabbed it from the kitchen and will put it back, but I will not stay inside."

"If you won't go inside, stay behind me," he said.

"You really think it's dangerous," she stated.

He glared at her in response, and she nodded, then fell behind him as he entered the fragrant rose garden as quietly as his bulky stature allowed.

"This is where I heard it," Gerard whispered.

Before Bella responded, a low growl sounded. A brown and white shape emerged from the bushes.

Gerard lifted the musket, aimed, and fired at the beast.

Chapter 24

Bellarose

*B*ang.

The wolf fell.

Bella dashed toward it.

Gerard leaped to grab her arm.

"Wait, it may still be alive. Injured animals are dangerous! Bella!"

She slipped out of his reach and got closer to the wolf.

The animal puffed out air through its nostrils and gazed up at them with azure human-like eyes. The ball had only hit the creature's hind leg, and blood seeped out of the wound. The animal growled a warning and Bella stopped.

"I won't hurt you." Her eyes welled with tears. "Let me help you," she whispered.

"Bella," Gerard said from behind her, "That injury isn't serious enough to disable it. "From my experience, wild animals have a high tolerance for pain. The wolf's survival instincts will kick in. We have to make sure it's dead before getting too close."

"Gerard, you're a monster." She choked on the words. "Why didn't you listen to me? He wasn't going to harm us."

The wolf's short tail thumped on the ground, and a whimper came from its throat.

"Look," she moved closer to the creature. "It's more afraid of us than we are of it."

It growled, and she stepped back again.

"You have no idea what this animal is capable of." Gerard approached cautiously. His voice sounded tighter, but not as if he were frightened. As if he were... sorry? "I should put it out of its misery."

"No!" She half turned and glowered at the tall man. "We're going to take it back to the stables and bandage it up so that it can heal."

Gerard shook his head, but his forehead was creased, though not in apparent anger "You can't keep this thing as a pet."

"I'm not talking about that. We can free it after the wound is mostly healed. We'll put it where it can't harm anyone." Bella's voice broke, and she swiped at the tears on her cheeks. "Maybe you can build a huge cage for it? One that can be transported when its leg is healed so we can move it far away from here?"

Gerard was still for a few seconds, then unfastened his belt.

Bella shifted her weight to protect the wolf. "What're you doing?"

"I'm going to secure the wolf so it can't bite me when I carry it to the barn."

She gaped up at the man who had been so unkind to her. "You'll... you'll do it? You'll help me save him?"

He bound the wolf's muzzle but wouldn't meet her gaze. "Can you use your shawl to bind his leg? I don't want to leave a trail of blood."

Without a second thought, Bella pulled off her shawl and wrapped it around the bleeding limb. Gerard squatted next to them but hesitated.

"He's not going to bite you."

"You don't know that. You can't read the animal's mind."

"He has kind eyes."

"You really are naïve. This is such a bad idea. Right then." Gerard picked up the wolf. "Oof! He's heavy."

Bella worried her lower lip. "He is rather large. Can you manage?"

Gerard cast her a scathing look. "Are you seriously asking me if I'm strong enough? Have you seen my muscles?"

She rolled her eyes.

"I can manage, but you will have to open the barndoors for me." After they'd gone half the distance, he said, "This thing obviously eats, which is the only reason you haven't been mauled to death yet."

When he tripped over a rock, the animal whimpered. Bella rushed to open the doors when they reached the stables,

Beautiful horses extended their noses over the stalls, and their nostrils flared. A chorus of anxious whinnies echoed. The enclosures were designed for them and not to imprison a wolf.

"This isn't going to work." Gerard grunted. "I can't build a cage before the creature will try to escape."

He might have a point, and putting the wolf in with a bunch of contained horses might be like tempting it with a feast at the dining table. Also, the horses seemed more agitated with the potential enemy as they stomped and neighed.

"It's too scared and injured to run away now." Bella pointed at the closest empty pen. "Put it over there."

Gerard glowered. "You obviously don't have any experience with wild animals, do you?"

"No, but this creature doesn't seem wild. Look at its eyes. They're like yours."

His lips curled partially. "You think I'm harmless?"

"Seriously? You're going to flirt with me *now*?" What was he thinking? The man was incorrigible. Bella blew out air. "I'm not interested. I don't know how much clearer I can be."

He chuckled but grew solemn as he placed the heavy wolf on top of the straw. The wolf's bleeding had slowed, but though it whined in pain, its azure eyes fastened on Gerard.

"I was jesting, Bella," he said, almost sadly. "You know, I was in love once. She's gone now, but the truth of it is, you aren't my Elayne."

His words drew all her attention from the wolf. "I... I'm sorry. But, then why—"

She broke off. His confession was like a wound in her own heart. Had all his bluster, arrogance, and flirtation been a way to hide from losing someone he cared about?

He shrugged. "It doesn't matter."

Bella harrumphed at him.

The wolf whined, drawing their attention back to it, and tried to stand, only to fall and whimper.

She approached the poor creature, but it cowered away. "We must do something to keep it from moving. it's only going to hurt itself."

"Aren't you the expert?" he asked with a touch of his caustic arrogance back in his voice. "What do you suggest?"

"We need to clean his injury, maybe remove that musket ball." Bella reached for the belt around the wolf's muzzle, but Gerard pulled her back. She shook off his hand. "Please take this off him. He's not going to bite."

Gerard shook his head.

Bella stood. "Fine. I'm going to find something to clean its wound." She headed toward the barn's exit.

"That's a bad idea. You'll probably make it angry."

"This wolf has every right to be livid after you tried to kill it." Bella slipped around Gerard's body blockade, but paused. "I wonder why there aren't any servants nearby. It's the middle of the day, but this place is empty. The horses are obviously cared for, but when does that happen and by whom?"

"Maybe it has to do with the enchantress's curse." Gerard kept his gaze on the wolf. "The more I think about the note the count—my father—wrote, the more I believe there has to be some kind of magical hex on this plantation. That would explain why this wolf isn't trying to rip us to shreds."

"No," she said. "I read that note, and it didn't say anything about cursing this place or the people living here."

"I know, but what if the lesson the enchantress tried to teach my parents when she kidnapped me didn't change them? They were afraid of her doing something worse, so they fled to Louisiana. What if something worse has happened here?"

The wolf gave a low, rumbling growl.

Bella jumped, and Gerard was immediately on high alert.

"Get back, Bella," he ordered, and for the first time, she believed he was once a young officer, giving commands.

She stepped against the wall while he searched the stables, returning with rope and extra planks. He cautiously approached the creature, which didn't try to escape while he tied a rope around its neck and to a metal hook on the stable wall. While Bella searched for a bucket of water for the wounded beast, he placed wood against the pen's opening. She handed him the bucket, and he set it close to the wolf, who watched him intently with those azure eyes. Gerard jumped over the barricade of planks and moved straw bales to prop them in place.

"That ought to be secure," he said. She gaped at him. He wasn't even winded, and his brow didn't show the slightest hint of sweat. "That wolf is too weak to push against all the weight. It won't get out, and the horses will be safe. I wonder if there's a paddock we could put them in so they aren't living in panic that a predator is in here with them.

"Well done," Bella conceded, "I think this will work for now, but you're right."

He bowed slightly. "So grand of you to point that out."

Somehow, this didn't spark her temper. She almost smiled. "We need a better solution until he heals. Being tied down is only going to make the wolf scared, and if he tries to escape, he could get injured even more."

"Not to mention that he'll spook the horses, even if he doesn't eat them." Gerard's blue eyes studied her, as if watching for a reaction. "No, the better solution would have been to let me kill the animal and put it out of its misery."

She groaned. "No, that is the cruel solution. Someone here must know how to care for injured animals. We need to find Brooke. I'll ask her to get the wolf some help."

"If all the horses end up murdered, I'm going to blame you," he said.

He had a point, maybe, but she raised her chin. "I believe the horses are safe for now."

They left the stable, and returned to the mansion. When they passed the study, Gerard hesitated.

"What is it?" she asked.

"Just thinking."

She bit back an unkind question about his abilities in thought. "Oh?"

"I'd planned on putting the musket back where I found it," he said slowly. "If that wolf escapes, or if it has a pack, and it comes after us... I think I'll hold onto the weapon instead. I won't let it hurt you, Bella, or anyone else, even if it means killing the wolf."

He continued down the hall, musket over his shoulder, leaving Bella stunned in the dim afternoon light.

Chapter 25

Wolf

He whimpered.

His hind leg burned with pain, and he was stuck.

The scent of panicked prey teased his nostrils, driving him to his feet again. He lunged at the dead wood locking him in, but it didn't move.

Panting, he tried to stand, to jump the sides of his cage and be free.

His leg crumpled, and he howled in pain.

Around him, horses stomped and whinnied.

But even if he left the human's trap, he couldn't break free from the flowers.

"Roses," a voice in his head said.

He growled to silence it, but that didn't change that this whole place was a snare. He'd never been able to leave and roam the forest. Something kept him close to the humans, even though people were dangerous.

His wound throbbed as a reminder of that fact.

A horse screamed and kicked. He rumbled a threat in response, but their fear grew stronger.

Slinking to the back of the trap, he curled around to chew at the human cloth around his leg. The scent of his own blood overpowered everything else. Blood and pain made him weak. His ears pricked, alert for whatever enemy might smell his weakness and make him a target, like the humans had.

They confused him. The small one—

"Woman... Bella," the man's voice whispered in his head. It was the voice that tried to control him and kept him from hurting the humans.

He yipped, and the voice fell quiet.

Bella. The short human. That one was gentle. The tall one had hurt him with that stick that barked thunder and smelled like... like...

"Gunpowder," said the man's voice inside his head.

His head rose up. How did a voice in his head know human things?

He tried to sit up again. Had to escape. Needed the trees and a place to hide.

But the trap the human had made was too strong. There was no way out.

He drank some water—though it tasted of horse—and tried to curl up and hide in the corner, behind the dead grass the humans had laid him on.

His heart pounded, but the pain left him tired and weak.

The sun was setting as he finally fell asleep.

Chapter 26

Gerard

No matter where Gerard and Bella searched, they didn't find a single person, and Bella was right, though he didn't want to admit it out loud. The longer they looked, the more unsettling he found all the cobwebs and dust. The entire mansion had been pristine and shiny only the night before.

Magic had to be the explanation, and he didn't like that reason at all.

Bella bit her lip. "Are you certain we didn't imagine everything that happened to us last night?"

Gerard rubbed his chin. "I'm absolutely certain. Both of us imagining the same thing is impossible."

Bella nodded in agreement, and they proceeded in unison. The drawn curtains remained opened, and late afternoon light illuminated the hallways. No one hid in the first rooms, but when they reached the third room on the left, Bella moved in front of him.

"This is the room I slept in last night," Bella whispered. "No one's in there."

"Why are you whispering and why did you shut the door?"

"There was... it was a mouse and I wanted to trap it."

"A mouse? You're afraid of a mouse but rush to help an injured wolf?" Gerard edged around her and turned the knob.

"You'll let it…" She gasped when the door swung open into a darkened room.

"I left the curtains open. I know I did!"

"I don't see any mice," Gerard teased.

She didn't respond. "I'm not going in there without a candle."

As if Bella had summoned it, the same candelabra Gerard dropped outside his bedroom earlier that day appeared on the floor. He jumped backward.

"Oh," Bella said, "I didn't see—"

"Bella, no!"

"Don't be silly, Gerard." She picked it up.

"Ouch! You have a tight grip."

Gerard's skin prickled.

Bella gasped. She dropped the golden candelabra and looked at Gerard in disbelief.

"Did that thing talk?"

He could only nod. He pinched his arm. If Bella saw and heard the same things, he wasn't hallucinating.

Very slowly, Bella knelt and picked it up again, but more gently. The candles lit, revealing a familiar face trapped inside the golden object. "Br-brooke?"

"Yes," the candelabra said, "you are looking at Brooke. I'm cursed, as is everyone on this plantation."

Bella's hands shook and the flames flickered.

"Please don't drop me," Brook-the-candelabra said quickly. "It hurts to land on the ground from so far up."

Wide-eyed, Gerard and Bella stared at each other, then at Brooke's tiny golden face. "I'm sorry to have startled you," she continued. "I wanted to tell you about the curse last night, but Antoine was against it. But please! Since so many of the objects in this estate are cursed, news has spread quickly that Gerard shot Antoine. You must bring him inside."

"No," Bella protested, "he shot a wolf."

The wolf's strange, blue eyes—No. That was ridiculous, even for magic. Gerard's hands threatened to shake, so he clenched them into fists. "I shot a dangerous animal, not my brother."

"Antoine is the wolf." Brooke's gold eyebrows knitted together. "The enchantress turned him into a beast to match his beastly behavior. There's no time to explain more now. We all go back to being human as evening approaches. We can discuss this then."

Bella squared her shoulders. "Gerard didn't know. He thought he was protecting everyone here."

For a moment her defense shored up his heart, but that didn't change the facts. "If I'd known," he said. He glared at the candelabra. "You should have told us."

Bella turned to him. "And I told you we should have left him be. He wouldn't have harmed us."

"That isn't necessarily true," Brooke said. "He's not able to think like a human when he's in that form. Unlike the rest of us, his mind changes along with his body."

A chill swept over Gerard. "And you want me to bring him inside where he could hurt people?"

"You must!" Worry was etched in Brook's metallic face. "If he dies, we have no hope of ever going back to our human state."

He crossed his arms. "I didn't shoot any vital organs—only his leg."

"Even a leg injury can lead to death. Surely as a soldier you know this!"

"I'm no surgeon," Bella interjected. "Neither is Gerard. I hate to point this out, but you aren't going to be able to help him in your current form."

"I can tell you what to do," Brooke pleaded. "Please hurry and get him."

His heart raced. He might not know his brother, who evidently didn't trust him and drugged him last night, but he wasn't going to lose him like he lost Elayne. Gerard pivoted and ran toward the stairs. Bella's lighter footsteps followed him.

"Oh dear, I think I'm going to change," Brooke exclaimed.

Gerard glanced over his shoulder. Bella stood at the bottom of the stairs, candelabra in hand.

"Please put me down." Brooke said. "Quickly!"

Bella placed the candelabra on the floor, and in a blink of an eye, Brooke appeared out of thin air, a lighted candlestick in her hand.

Gerard blinked several times. "Bella, tell me you saw that too."

"I did," Bella admitted in a small voice. "Magic…"

As if a magical transformation were ordinary, Brooke hoisted her skirts and ran. "Hurry! We don't have time! We need to see if Antoine is alright!"

When they reached the barn, they all heard Antoine shouting.

"Oh dear," Brooke muttered between gasps of air.

Antoine yelled, "Brooke! Someone! Help!" A low groan interrupted his calls, then he said, "I'm bleeding!"

Gerard threw open the doors and thundered to the boarded-up stall. There, in the bloodied straw, lay his brother, stark naked. Bella charged up behind him.

"We're coming, Antoi—" She let out a shriek and spun around, her back to the stall. "Gerard," she whispered frantically. "He's got nothing on! Brooke! He's not wearing anything at all!"

Brooke, who lingered at the barn door, said, "Of course not."

"Oh my!"

Torn between amusement, guilt, and determination, Gerard grabbed a horse blanket and tossed it over his brother's body. He shoved aside the bales of hay, moved the boards, and then untied the ropes.

Antoine glowered up at him and said several choice curse words in French.

Gerard smirked. His brother wasn't such a well-mannered gentleman after all.

"Gerard," Antoine asked in English, "where is Brooke? Why am I tied up, and why is my leg bleeding?"

"I thought you were a danger to the estate, so I shot you."

"You *shot* me?"

"Yes," Gerard said as calmly as he could. "In my defense, you were a wolf and very close to the plantation. Wolves don't venture around people unless they're up to no good. My experience with wolves is that they attack livestock, or even people." He met his brother's angry gaze. "You were way too close to the house. It was my duty to protect it and all the people inside."

"I told you we should have explained the curse to them." Brooke called out.

Antoine cursed and gained composure before responding. "I see that now, but I really do try to control the wolf from harming anyone." He hugged the blanket around himself, and calmly said, "Ladies, would you please go back to the house so I can find my clothes?"

Bella didn't need to be asked twice. She darted out of the stable with Brooke right behind her. Gerard chuckled inwardly. She acted tough and worldly, but she was a sheltered aristocrat's daughter in the end.

He turned back to Antoine and held out a hand.

"Let's get you inside, brother, and tend to your wound." He drew a deep breath and added, "For what it's worth, I'm sorry."

Chapter 27

Brooke

B rooke and Bella found Antoine's discarded garments on the path to the house near the woodpile.

Brooke ran close enough to the barn for Antoine to hear. "I found your clothes. I'll leave them outside the doors and Gerard can help you dress."

She caught up to Bella and they went back to the kitchen to gather medical supplies. They brought them to the library and covered the settee with blankets before Gerard helped Antoine into the room. Bella blushed scarlet and fled, and Brooke shooed Gerard after her.

"Where were you shot?" she asked, somehow managing to keep the tremor out of her voice.

"It's not as bad as I feared," Antoine said. "Just the side of my calf."

Gratitude swept through Brooke.

"That should be easy to mend," she said. If it had hit a different spot... Well, there was the benefit that Antoine wouldn't have to take off his britches for her to reach the wound. "I'm thankful we don't need to call a physician."

"Me too." He offered her a smile as he pulled off what looked like a woman's shawl, a temporary bandage. He set his leg on the blankets. "I'd hate to have an outsider involved in our... unusual situation."

She knelt beside him and gently investigated the wound. "I believe the musket ball was pushed out when you transformed from beast to man." For several minutes she worked on the injury. "We need to tell Bella and Gerard everything."

"You're right." Antoine sighed. "We should go down and eat with them and explain all of this."

"There. Your leg is clean and bandaged. I'll redress it tomorrow, but when you're a wolf, neither of us can keep your leg clean."

"I know." He pulled his sock up and tied the garter around it. "Brooke, I changed before twilight ended yesterday."

She frowned. "I didn't see you, but I also changed before the normal time."

"It seems I'm spending less time as a human the closer I get to my nineteenth birthday."

"Then we really need to get your brother and Bella involved," she said. "I believe they can help us."

He sat quietly while she tucked the soiled cloths and her supplies into a basket.

"Are you ready?"

He slid on his shoes and nodded. "It's improbable that my selfish brother and a jaded bankrupt aristocrat girl could free us from this curse." His forehead wrinkled. "I'm sorry I've made life unbearable for you and the others."

As much as Brooke should still be angry at Antoine's former selfish behavior, she smiled softly and touched his arm. "It's all right," she murmured. "I—we—know you've changed." She pinched her lips closed before she added, *I forgive you.*

Antoine put his hand over hers. "Thank you, Brooke." As if he suddenly realized that he was touching her, he yanked his hand back. "You... you always know just what to say."

Antoine wobbled a little when he stood. Brooke walked at his side, in case he needed to lean on her shoulder. Together, they made their way toward the delicious smells drifting from the dining room. Brooke felt Gerard and Bella's stares as they approached the table.

"Due to the unusual circumstances, I've asked Brooke to eat with us." Antoine pulled out the chair for her to sit next to Bella who had moved over for Brooke to face Gerard.

"We need answers," Gerard demanded as soon as Antoine was seated at the head of the table.

"We'll tell you everything. I was foolish for not sharing with you last night," Antoine confessed. "You see, our parents never learned their lesson, not even after you were taken from them, and I'm afraid I followed their example. I was as arrogant and cruel as they were." He rested his elbows on the table. "I thought that behavior was normal—anyone who wasn't an aristocrat didn't deserve my kindness. Even those who shared a similar status and wealth only received a minimum amount of respect from me."

Antoine put his head into his hands. Brooke touched his shoulder. He had to be exhausted from the pain and the ever longer nights as a wolf. Bella and Gerard remained silent.

Antoine raised his head and met his brother's gaze. "Moving to Louisiana was pointless. Aerowyn found us and disguised herself as one of the slaves who worked in the fields. I scolded her for coming into the mansion since she wasn't a house slave." He looked down at his plate. "When she transformed into herself... it was the first time I knew anything about magic and the enchantress."

Gerard scowled, "She is deceitful."

"Perhaps, but she wasn't wrong." Antoine continued, "Aerowyn explained she had visited my parents before and warned them about their behavior. She didn't explain how she had punished them, only told me that she had cautioned them to change their ways or I would suffer a worse fate."

He paused.

"Go on," Bella urged softly.

"That's when my body tore apart as my bones and muscles took on a different shape."

Bella gasped, and Gerard leaned forward. Brooke kept her hand on Antoine's shoulder.

"For those first minutes, I'm aware of what's going on. I saw my hands become paws, watched my nose stretch. But I thought it was just me. It wasn't until I woke up naked, Brooke at my side, that I realized we were all cursed."

Bella squeaked.

Gerard's eyebrows lowered. He glanced at Brooke, then leveled a glare at his brother, "What does that mean?"

Antoine's cheeks pinkened. "She found me."

"I saw him change," Brooke clarified, and though her face heated, she held Gerard's gaze until he nodded slowly.

"She told me that when I transformed into another living creature, the people in the mansion took on the shapes of objects found in the plantation and stables." Antoine swallowed hard. "Brooke told me that as soon as I turned into a wolf, she became the candelabra. The only difference between my hex and everyone else's was that those who became objects were able to use their senses and understood what happened to them."

"Antoine doesn't agree," Brooke added, "but Aerowyn protected us from Antoine by enchanting us too. If we had remained human, he could have harmed or killed us. When he is a wolf—" she drew a deep breath "—I am too frightened to run."

His jaw tightened. "I don't blame her. The first time I transformed into the wolf, I was caged inside the house. Between the wolf's confusion and fear, I caused a lot of damage. After that first night, I knew what to expect. But despite my human side fighting to reason with the animal, the wolf normally wins, and my humanity continually moves in and out of consciousness."

"Some of the enchanted furniture needed bandages after they became human, but their wounds would have been much worse had they remained people." Brooke said.

"But you didn't attack me," Bella put in suddenly. "How is it that you didn't hurt me or Gerard after he shot you?"

"After that first day, I knew when the beast was ready to emerge. I went outside, into the woods, to avoid destroying the inside of the house or hurting anyone. I take my clothes off next to the forest entrance, but yesterday, there wasn't time to place them neatly in their usual spot." His face reddened again. "I always end up there because the wolf's instinct to flee into the forest loses to my desire to be near home as twilight approaches."

"We all feel the change coming on, but we can't predict it. We believe it has something to do with the sun setting, because before it gets completely dark, our bodies experience the tingling of magic." Brooke rubbed her arms. "We're only human for a few hours every night. It's the time you can see the atmospheric rays in the sky."

Gerard leaned back in his chair. "Did Aerowyn give you any way to break this spell?"

"She explained the hex would become permanent on my nineteenth birthday. I would become immortal, along with everyone cursed on the plantation. I'd be a wolf and everyone else would be an object forever." Antoine looked down at his hands. "The only way I can end it is to find unselfish love."

Gerard closed his eyes and blew out a huge sigh. "That is like commanding the sun when to shine. I felt that kind of love once." His jaw stiffened. "She's gone now."

"That doesn't mean your brother can't find his true love," Bella said.

"It's not necessarily a romantic type of love, like in fairy tales." Brooke explained. "The enchantress said unselfish love."

Gerard whispered, "I can't," then stood abruptly. "Well, knowing this place is full of talking objects for all eternity, I think I'm better off living above The Swan."

Bella stood up, too, though she was much shorter than he was.

"Gerard," the tiny young woman commanded. "Stop being self-centered!"

Gerard laughed, but he didn't look amused. "You can't prevent me from leaving, but your pathetic attempt is humorous. Give me a good reason to stay."

"Your brother." Bella stated.

"As you've pointed out before, I don't care about anyone but my-self."

"You did once." Her voice grew gentle. "I can see it in your eyes. I hear it in your voice."

Gerard winced and looked away. Hope flickered in Brooke's heart. Bella had hit a nerve.

Then his face hardened. "Why do you care what happens to these people? They aren't your family."

Grief washed over Bella's demeanor. "Because I have no family and I have nowhere to go. Yes, I'm better off here, trying to break their curse, than living on the street and begging for food or shelter. But even if it doesn't profit me at all, I'd still offer my help." She placed her hand on his arm. "Please Gerard, for the sake of your lost love, whoever she was, help break the spell."

Gerard's expression changed again. Brooke held her breath. Maybe he would stay. Maybe the two of them could break the hex.

As quick as the thought hit, sadness followed. Gerard *had* lost his true love. Maybe his bluster was only to cover up what he truly felt—who he really was underneath.

"If I stay, I need you to know that if the curse doesn't get broken, that it isn't my fault. I don't have any control over this wretched spell." He crossed his arms. "The real enemy is Aerowyn—not me!"

Bella's exuberant smile returned. "Perhaps it is a result of me reading so many books with happy endings, but I think we can defeat the enchantment. Or maybe it is because I haven't eaten this well since I don't know when. Either way, I'm taking this seriously."

"You like books?" Antoine asked suddenly.

Brooke shook her head. "Don't change the subject."

"What more is there to talk about?" Antoine said. "We're cursed."

Bella exhaled loudly. "But how did the enchantress expect you to find love if you're a wolf longer than you're a human?"

"I don't know. Aerowyn didn't explain anything other than the fact that I was a beast and needed to be taught a lesson." Antoine offered Brooke a faint smile. "Trust me, I have changed my perspective on how I look at people—rich or poor, but I don't exactly have the opportunity to build relationships during the short time I'm a human."

Brooke's cheeks warmed, but she hoped no one saw it.

"Antoine, we've all noticed your improvements." She turned to Bella. "I was only a lowly servant of the estate and Antoine promoted me. Now I manage most of his personal and financial affairs."

Her smile widened as she reflected on how he trusted her with all his secrets. Antoine's faith in her only increased her attraction to him. She folded her napkin into a precise triangle and set it aside, but if only she could set aside her feelings as easily. Antoine would never reciprocate her affection. Sometimes, though, the heart wanted something it couldn't have.

"Can anyone who lives here love you and break the spell?"

Bella's question brought Brooke's attention back to the present. The young woman was staring straight at her. Brooke's face warmed.

"Another good question," Antoine said. "Sadly, I don't think it can."

Dejection tinted with resentment filtered through Brooke. She took a swallow of water and said, "Antoine might be right. It hasn't broken so far, even though we have all grown close."

The longer the curse remained, the more she knew her feelings weren't enough to break Aerowyn's spell. Wouldn't true love need to be shared? What if her love was too selfish? After all, the promise of never being a candelabra again could taint her motivation, couldn't it?

Brooke was saved from her whirling thoughts and emotions for Antoine when Mrs. Watson's daughter, Emma, came scurrying into the dining room with a cart of dessert and tea.

"Hello everyone!"

The girl curtsied. "I'm excited to finally make your acquaintance, Miss Bella. My name is Emma."

"You are the voice in my bedroom!" Bella exclaimed. When Emma nodded, Bella grinned. "You frightened me! I thought I was hearing things and I saw your face in the canopy frame."

Mrs. Watson waddled in. "Miss Bella, I'm sorry. I worried that putting you into that room was a mistake, but I wanted you to have some pretty clothes."

"You lied to me!" Gerard said suddenly. "You said that you were afraid of a mouse, but you were afraid of talking furniture!"

Bella shot him a glare. "Mrs. Watson, you shouldn't forgive Gerard for interrupting. He has ghastly manners."

Mrs. Watson nervously clasped her hands.

Antoine dipped his head. "Please continue, Mrs. Watson."

She glanced at Gerard before continuing. "The problem is that the enchantress didn't give any thought to who became what in this house. I think our inhuman forms were based on what we were nearest to at the time the spell was cast. Emma was dusting the bed posts at the time. But please forgive her, Miss Bella. She is only seven years old and this all has been especially hard on her."

Brooke's opinion of Bella grew when the young woman stood and crossed to the girl.

"It's quite alright. I can only imagine. When I was your age, I was climbing trees and playing in the mud."

Emma's dimpled smile couldn't be contained as she curtsied again.

Mrs. Watson patted Emma on the head. "We'll be leaving the tea, Sir."

"Thank you," Antoine said.

"Come along, Emma."

"Well done, Bella." Antoine said in a quiet, pleased voice, and Bella blushed. "Emma is a spirited girl, but is picky about who she befriends. She must like you."

A twinge of jealousy made Brooke tense. If Bella gained Antoine's affections, she may be the one to break the curse. She pushed the resentment aside realizing releasing the plantation from its spell was more important than her love life.

Her dreams of finding love with Antoine were far-fetched anyway.

Chapter 28

Gerard

At mid-morning Gerard drove a smaller carriage into New Orleans to meet with Monsieur Alexandre before the man returned to France. Bella asked if he'd take her to The Swan when she discovered he was going. He chose a vehicle he knew wasn't cursed, so their conversation was private. Not that they would say anything that required secrecy, but Gerard didn't like the feeling of being spied on.

Gerard offered his hand to help Bella into the coach. "Who are you going to meet?"

She wore a pale green, long flowing, cotton dress adorned with intricate white ribbons.

"My friend Quinn."

Bella's cheeks reddened.

"I didn't know you had any friends at The Swan."

"Only one. Why do you need to go into town?" Bella asked.

"I'm giving Father's lawyer, Monsieur Alexandre, a letter from Antoine stating he accepts the legal responsibility of half of Rose Manor's estate." Gerard picked up the horses' reins and clicked his tongue. "Antoine didn't want to risk turning into a wolf in front of the man to sign the legal documents of Father's will, so we hope this will be adequate."

The black horses took off and trotted down the road stirring up scents of the red soil that blended nicely with nearby pine trees. It reminded Gerard of his first journey to Rose Manor and all the questions he had about his brother. He didn't know much about Antoine because of the short time he spent as a man.

Gerard asked, "What do you think of Antoine?"

"Despite the week of evenings with him, I don't know if I can have an accurate opinion."

"Do you think he's handsome?" Gerard glanced over to see her reaction.

Bella blushed. "Yes, but…"

"But what?"

"I don't really know him. I think a man's real attractiveness shines when their personality is kind, generous, and delightful."

"There you go talking about me again." Gerard turned his head to wink in jest.

She teased back, "You really have a high opinion of yourself, don't you?" Then she laughed. "I know we had a rough introduction to each other, but it's nice that we're able to move past that."

"On a more serious note, I struggle with conflicting emotions over my brother. Since we're away from prying ears, I thought your perspective might help me." Gerard turned his head and shock was written on Bella's face.

"I didn't think I would ever hear you ask for my opinion."

Gerard chuckled. "I promise I won't make a habit of it. The thing is Aerowyn's manipulations in my life has me conflicted."

"What about?"

"I can't help but resent Antoine for having it all, and yet I'm grateful that I avoided the worst of Aerowyn's hex. My adopted parents loved me, but we suffered a lot." He straightened. "Would I have been able to stop Aerowyn from hurting my family?" He turned his head to see Bella briefly frown.

"I'm the wrong person to ask." She paused and then let her opinions flow. "I have seen improvement on how you treat people, but I remember your behavior at The Swan. Despite the loss you've experienced, I don't think your behavior would have been excused. I doubt you could have changed the enchantress' mind from hexing the plantation."

Gerard knew he was a better man than Antoine. Before the war he had been selfless enough to appease the angry enchantress. Afterall, he had served his country, provided for his family, loved and lost, but what had Antoine done? Nothing. He sat on his wealth, comfortable and provided for. And, it wasn't that Bella mattered, but it was a constant irritation that while she had been so rude to Gerard, she treated Antoine so respectfully. True, she'd been less abrasive lately, but she was still more pleasant around Antoine.

His behavior had changed after the war. The encounter with the witch Aerowyn, whether real or some hallucination like a nightmare, only brought his suffering to light. What would an enchantress know about battle? About loss? Surely her magic could give her anything she wanted.

"Bella, you're right. You aren't the correct person to ask." He glanced over to see her frown. "You didn't know me before the war. I did my best to provide for my family in France, while Antoine didn't have any responsibilities. I went hungry. Antoine never did."

"That must have been difficult." Bella's voice broke. "Since I left France, I have become familiar with what it feels like to be hungry."

The two sat in silence until Bella was dropped off at the stables where Gerard briefly saw the hunchbacked young man, she told him about.

"I'll return as soon as my business is complete." He shook the reins and the carriage moved onto the hotel.

Pondering over their conversation and Aerowyn's spell, Gerard thought it was hard to imagine caring enough to sacrifice himself for anyone except Elayne, so Bella had to be the one to break Antoine's hex. Did he hope Quinn was only a friend? Ironically, it made him a little envious imagining Bella with his brother.

Why should Antoine end up with true love? What made Antoine more worthy than himself?

Gerard hadn't been able to stop from falling in love, so he wouldn't be able to prevent his brother from falling for Bella. He scowled. Although... if the curse became permanent, he would be the master of the whole estate. Or maybe he could take the monetary portion of his inheritance now and leave.

But Bella's earlier words about him caring for someone in his past haunted him. Another missed lifetime, like being stolen from wealth to grow up in hunger. It simply wasn't fair.

"Not fair!" he said suddenly as he held the reins a little tighter.

After the business with Monsieur Alexandre was completed, he headed back to The Swan's stables. Bella waited for him. They sat in silence except for Bella's humming. She was grinning too—none of this was her normal. Was it Quinn? Should he care if it impacted Rose Manor's hexed people?

When they arrived back at the plantation, Gerard put the carriage away and took care of the horses. He went into the mansion afterward and wandered the cobwebbed halls. Slabs of light fell through the dingy windows. He checked the tall, standing clock, only to find it wasn't working. Well, it would be twilight soon enough, and he'd have to deal with Antoine again.

When he neared the library, he heard women's voices, and after a moment, he ignored his conscience and angled himself to see through the partially opened double-doors but still be hidden from view. After all, he needed information.

Brooke's candles were fully lit as she was on top of a table near Bella who worked a needlepoint.

"What do you want to do once the spell is broken?" Brooke was saying.

"I hoped Antoine and Gerard would allow me to stay here. I could be a maid, or something else useful, with the proper training." Bella paused. "Why do you ask?"

"I'm sure the master can find a suitable position for you, but..."

"Go on."

"I was wondering if perhaps there is another reason you found your way here. Don't you find it strange that the old lady vanished right after telling you this plantation needed servants?" Brooke's candles flickered out. "I think she was the enchantress leading you here to help break the curse."

Was she upset? Gerard leaned closer to the door. If she was, that made no sense. The only way they would all go back to being humans was if Antoine found his true love.

Bella's cheeks turned rosy, and she waited a long time before she said anything, which was odd. Had he ever seen Bella at a loss for words before?

"Maybe. But maybe the enchantress wanted me to have a home. It's not that I don't find Antoine attractive, but—well—there's someone else."

Brooke perked up and her candles blazed again.

"What do you mean?"

Bella continued working busily on her embroidery. "When I arrived in New Orleans, I met Quinn."

That's why Bella was humming. Gerard couldn't deny her mood was almost joyous.

"He's Gustave's—the owner's—son." Bella's voice changed, as if she was angry. "Gustave makes Quinn do the hard work outside to keep him away from the tavern patrons. He's ashamed of his son."

"Why?"

"He's not like other people." Bella put her project down and smiled. "But he's so kind. After I learned of the curse, Mrs. Watson sent me to town on errands, and I was able to tell Quinn that I found a new home and job. I had to leave The Swan without talking to him, so when I disappeared, he worried about me. He... he was my protector when the tavern customers got rough. Quinn was even teaching me to sword fight. He said that I needed to be able to protect myself." She sighed. "Today I joined Gerard when he went to town so that I could visit Quinn. I take every opportunity available to see him."

Brooke tilted, but then righted herself before falling. "You didn't answer my question. Why would Quinn's father hide him from everyone?"

"He has a humped back."

"Oh..."

Gerard's forehead wrinkled. She wasn't blind to his deformity, but why was she attracted to him?

"He walks hunched over because of it." Bella said, a hint of anger in her voice when she continued, "I don't like the way his father treats him. He deserves love."

This new revelation angered Gerard. Beautiful, stuck-up Bellarose preferred an undersized stable boy to him? She had ignored him at The Swan because she was more interested in a boy too ugly to be seen in public? Gerard ground his teeth, and it took him a moment to refocus on the women's conversation.

"Quinn sounds like a fine young man," Brooke said quietly.

"Oh, he is." Bella's smile disappeared. "I know this must be disappointing, but I don't think I can break the enchantment over this plantation."

"Well, you can't force yourself to love someone," Brooke said peppily. "If you don't care for Master Antoine in that way, the curse couldn't be broken."

"How do *you* feel about Antoine?" Bella asked cautiously.

The candelabra's face changed from gold to copper.

"What do you mean?" Brooke's voice went up a pitch. "I'm a servant. Master Antoine is my employer." Her voice softened. "Although, before the spell was cast, I didn't care for his arrogant behavior, he's changed drastically. I don't hate him like I did."

"You seemed relieved I was interested in someone else."

Brooke sputtered, then said, "I'm only happy for you."

"And it had nothing to do with the fact that you were relieved that Antoine and I wouldn't be falling in love?"

"Oh my, it's nearly twilight!" Brooke exclaimed. "It's almost time for us to all go back to being human."

Bella chuckled, and Gerard backed into the hall. It wouldn't do for them to know he'd been eavesdropping.

His stomach rumbled, and he turned toward the kitchen. Gerard noticed through the windows the sky was painted in hues of orange, pink, purple, and blue as the sun dipped below the horizon. Antoine would be returning soon, and dinner would be prepared. Yes, he and Bella ate left-overs every day, but he was always famished by the time the house returned to normal.

So, Brooke cared for Antoine outside a servant's loyalty to her master? Could she break the curse, or was there time? Antoine's nineteenth birthday—their nineteenth birthday—was quickly approaching.

After all, he had fallen in love with Elayne in a shorter amount of time. He would have died in her place, if the fates had allowed him that option. An ache swelled in his chest, and he tried to shove it away. Maybe it wasn't as impossible as it seemed.

Feeling the need to bury the pain more than satisfy his hunger, he went outside to chop wood. Eventually, the swing of the ax and the heat in his arms burned away emotions and thought.

Chapter 29

Bellarose

How had Bella not seen it before? Brooke loved Antoine.

After Brooke hopped out of the library, her golden face still flushed copper, Bella paced. While Antoine, Brooke, and the rest of the staff had been stuck in this curse, Brooke had become more of a partner than a servant. She ungrudgingly helped Antoine with everything. The fact that they got along so well should have been all the sign Bella had needed.

It made sense once Bella thought about it. When Quinn was the only friend she had in a strange town, they bonded over their similar circumstances. He was ostracized from people in a town he lived in all his life. He understood the loneliness she had felt.

Even today, Bella attempted to ignore the feelings she was developing for him. Her faced warmed as she recalled how Quinn had beamed when he asked, "What brings you into town?" And then added quickly, "I don't mind seeing you, but I didn't expect you so soon after your last visit."

The words were simple enough, but Bella was elated over the fact that she had made him smile. His happiness to see her after their separation, woke up feelings she had tried to bury. Sometimes you can't stop your heart from caring, and maybe that is what had happened to Brooke.

Although, they hadn't broken the curse yet. Maybe Brooke's love wasn't enough. Bella strode between the walls of the library contemplating why.

Maybe Brooke was too busy managing an enchanted household as a candlestick?

She crossed her arms.

Maybe Antoine was too busy recovering from being an animal?

She stopped and adjusted a crooked painting on the wall.

Maybe it was too late for them to fall in love?

Eventide had fallen when soiled, sweaty, and unwanted, Gerard entered the library.

"What have you been doing?" Bella scrunched her nose. "You look like you've been rolling around in the dirt."

"And a hello to you too." Gerard mock bowed. "I was chopping wood. I must keep my muscles finely tuned in case I meet a helpless damsel who needs my assistance."

"Really?" She coughed to cover a laugh. "Are there a lot of ladies around here who need your help?"

"You never know." He flashed her a toothy grin. "I was off to clean up, but thought I'd check to see if any of the furniture had become humans in here."

Bella tilted her head. "Are you looking for someone in particular?"

"No. I only wanted to know because I didn't want anyone spying on me in my room. It's a little unnerving to be unsure which objects are hexed people." His brows knitted together.

"I know what you mean, but in my room, only Emma is there to observe me."

"What if the curse doesn't break? The house will be full of objects who were once human and Antoine will become a wild animal that will either need to be killed or moved away from here."

An expression washed over Gerard's face that Bella couldn't read. Since he had trusted her earlier with his conflicting emotions, she shared with him the conversation she had with Brooke.

She fidgeted with her hair. "Brooke thought I was sent here to break the curse, but I can't."

"The thought crossed my mind too, but why can't you?" Gerard looked Bella in the eyes.

"I may have fallen in love—" She quickly slapped her palm over her mouth.

"You may have fallen in love with who?"

Her insides warmed unnaturally. "I don't know if it's exactly love, but I have strong feelings for someone I first met when coming to New Orleans."

Gerard gave a crooked grin. "I'm shocked that it's not me."

"Even if I hadn't started to care deeply for another man before you came along, you're not my type." Bella lightly bit her lip.

"I feel the same way about you. With our first encounter, you may have thought I wanted you for love, but I wasn't looking for anything long term." He lifted his eyebrows. "Anyway, who is this person you care about too much to be charmed by my obvious superiority?"

Bella said softly, "Quinn, Gustave's son."

"The stable boy you met with today?" Gerard chortled. "That explains so much. If he's kind to you, there must be something wrong with him." After a pause, he clarified, "When I say 'wrong', I'm not talking about his back. Only his judgment of women."

His mischievous smile prevented her from becoming angry. If she had a brother, he would have probably teased her like Gerard.

Bella glowered at him in pretend rage. "You're infuriating!"

It took time to move past their first impressions of each other, but they had finally come to an understanding. He pretended to be arrogant and she acted outraged. Their lively banter may have seemed rude to an outsider, but for them, it was a way to distract them from becoming too melancholy over past hurts.

With quick wit Gerard responded, "That's the kettle calling the pot black." Gerard laughed. "No, really, what is it about this Quinn that makes you care?"

The words tumbled out freely. "Quinn is like no one I have ever met before. When I first walked off the ship, I was scared—like a fish out of water. Men tried to take advantage of me being alone without a chaperone, but Quinn swept in and protected me, at the risk of being ridiculed."

"I could have protected you—"

Bella shook her head. "You weren't there."

He sat down, oblivious to how much work it would take to clean the fine fabric. "I could have."

"But Quinn did. Most people either avoid him because of his appearance or make fun of him. Some people think he has a contagious disease, which only makes them crueler towards Quinn."

Gerard's fingers traced along his chin contemplatively. "I see that your affection for Quinn simply can't be contained."

She held her hand over her heart. "No, because I know that his appearance doesn't matter." She grinned. "Besides, he taught me how to sword fight and doesn't care that I'm a poor aristocrat girl. My past doesn't bother him at all."

"I have trouble picturing you two dueling with swords. How does an inn keeper's son learn how to sword fight?" Gerard mocked. "The image of you and the deformed man incompetently knocking swords together in combat is now rolling around in my head."

"Quinn is not incapable! Since he runs his father's stables, he became a blacksmith. He doesn't only make horseshoes, but also has become a genius at molding metal into beautiful weapons," Bella gushed. "Captains, sailors, and privateers come from all over the world to commission Quinn to make them special swords. After a while, he asked for blade combat lessons for payment, since his father stole all the money anyway. He taught me a few of the basics, and he practices every chance he gets. He'll leave home and become a sailor one day, but for now, he trains."

Gerard eyed her for several minutes, then gave a low whistle. "I admit it. I didn't expect someone like you to care for an outcast. I guess that means you're not the answer to ending the curse. I certainly don't want to live here if everything is hexed. I'm tired of hallucinations and talking objects."

Briefly, the question of what delusions haunted him flitted through Bella's mind, but she only said, "I think there is another girl who might be Antoine's potential true love."

"Let me guess," he said. "Brooke."

Her eyes widened. "You thought so too?"

He shrugged. "I've thought if she wasn't a candleholder most of the time, I would try to hook up with her for a distraction. After all, I'm much more handsome than Antoine."

Bella studied him a moment, decided he jested, and said mildly, "You really are a cad! No, I suspect she has feelings for your brother and is afraid to admit it."

Gerard turned serious. "What would it take to get those two together?"

Bella tucked in her lips. This was a chance to force Antoine and Brooke together, but she didn't want to sound foolish. "Well... I was thinking just now that perhaps we could throw a ball and get all the prominent citizens of New Orleans to attend. If Brooke isn't meant for Antoine, then perhaps another beautiful girl will show up who is."

"A ball? I bet you read that in one of your silly books," Gerard scoffed.

"Yes, I did, but that doesn't matter. I think it could work."

He scratched his chin thoughtfully. "Probably not, but maybe another woman could be used to get Brooke jealous. That'd force her to admit that she likes Antoine."

"That isn't the point, Gerard! That idea could backfire." She drew in a breath. "I think it would be better to get the two of them to dance."

Gerard laughed outright.

"It could work. They would look into each other's eyes, and—"

He gagged. "You read too many love stories. That's not how people fall in love."

"I'm sure you're experienced in the matter," Bella said hotly.

His humor evaporated. "As a matter of fact, I am."

Too stunned by his admittance, Bella stood, mouth open as he stormed from the library.

She had to have been right about him loving someone, though she still had no idea who. Maybe he had been a very different person, long ago.

Nevertheless, Bella knew the dance floor was the perfect setting for falling in love. All she needed to do was convince Antoine and Brooke a ball could break the spell.

Chapter 30

Antoine

Antoine approached the library and was almost knocked over by Gerard.

"Brother, I didn't see you." Gerard stopped moving. "How has the world been treating you today?"

"I am well, despite my beastly tendencies." Antoine bowed slightly. Gerard became solemn.

"My past behavior towards Bella would have shamed my parents." Antoine blinked. That came out of nowhere. "Our parents?"

"Mine. They were the kindest, most unselfish people I knew. Even when they had way too many mouths to feed, they fed a beggar who knocked at our door."

His brother's words sank in. Hesitantly, Antoine asked, "Did you ever go hungry?"

"Sometimes. My parents scrounged up at least one meal a day." Gerard's eyes moistened, and he turned away. "The king sent them my pay, but I hope someday to send them enough to truly improve their lives, not just pay off debts."

Antoine cleared his throat, then slapped him on the back. "Well, you're rich now! Send them whatever you want. This estate belongs to both of us."

"I'm concerned about the curse." Gerard turned and met Antoine's gaze. "What will happen if you stay a wolf?"

Antoine shifted his weight. "If my predicament becomes permanent, all of this belongs to you alone."

"I still would need help running this plantation."

"I suppose as long as the servants are under the hex, they can't help." Antoine rubbed his temples. "I can't manage the estate when I spend most of my time as a wolf. That's why your presence is so valuable."

Gerard clenched his jaw. "I know how to run a small farm to feed one family, not an entire plantation."

"That might be true, but if the hex isn't broken, I can teach you in the time I have left." Antoine inwardly begged Gerard to agree, but stated with confidence he didn't quite feel, "This can work."

"I'm not even convinced this is the life I want."

Antoine winced. If Gerard wasn't willing to learn, the family plantation would be lost.

Gerard scrubbed a hand over his eyes. "Besides, there isn't enough time to train me adequately—that is, if we don't break the spell."

Antoine slumped. "You mean, if *I* don't break the spell. It is my fault we are worrying about it in the first place." He straightened. "Brooke can help you, too, since she can still talk in her cursed form. She's a valuable asset."

"Yes, but how long can we keep that up?" Gerard tensed. "Eventually, I will have to hire more help—help that *doesn't* change into inanimate objects. How could I explain this situation to any outsiders without scaring them? You need to find your true love, and fast."

Antoine massaged the back of his neck. "Our birthday is two weeks away. No one falls in love that fast."

"I did."

Antoine's eyes widened. "You? When?"

A wistfulness fell over Gerard's features. "I met an American officer's daughter during the war. She volunteered to help with the wounded soldiers. Her name was Elayne." His usually aggressive stance softened. "She was beautiful and kind, but full of spirit. She helped my best friend, Leo, after he lost his leg. I knew I loved her the first day I met her, but I had to wait for her to notice I existed. She kept me humble and didn't allow my accomplishments in the war to make me arrogant.

"What happened to her?" Antoine asked quietly.

Gerard's face fell. "She was killed in a British raid. I have nightmares about the war. One is of when I found her dead on the ground, bleeding. I vowed to never love again after that."

As if suffering from hunger on a farm with a poor family wasn't enough? Antoine shuddered. Losing someone he loved would have been one hundred times worse. Visions of Brooke on that hard ground punctured his heart, and at that moment, Antoine knew he loved her. But could she love him? She knew him before he had reformed his ways.

Still, he hadn't lost everything yet—but his brother had. Over and over. Antoine clasped Gerard's shoulder. "We can't rationalize love." Antoine's emotions stirred. "But you shouldn't give up on the idea of it. Elayne must have been wonderful, but perhaps someday you will love another."

Gerard blinked rapidly, and a knot formed in Antoine's throat.

Then, Gerard straightened. "I'm famished. Do you know when the food will be ready? Waiting for the kitchen to turn human each day has been a challenge for me. Perhaps we could hire a kitchen staff for during the day?"

Antoine shook his head and chuckled. Of course, the war hero wasn't going to show his emotions—not even to his brother. "I can change the subject as easily as you, but before we eat, I want to confess something to you." He swallowed and said, "I love Brooke." He heaved out a loud breath. "That is the first time I admitted it out loud."

Before Gerard could comment on Antoine's words, Brooke appeared in the hallway.

"Dinner is ready," she said.

The brothers exchanged a look.

"I'll be right there. I've got to clean up first. Go on." He turned and jogged down the hall, then stopped and turned around. "Antoine."

"Yes?"

"Don't waste any more time. All you have is right now."

The door clicked as Gerard closed it behind him, leaving Antoine alone in the hall with Brooke, the woman Antoine loved. Her life also had been ruined when the enchantress hexed him.

"Monsieur Antoine?" Brooke's gentle smile brought one of his own.

He offered her his arm. "Dinner, then?"

She blushed but slid her small hand onto his arm. It wasn't really enough to make Antoine believe she had feelings for him, but what if she did?

Maybe, just maybe, there was hope for the spell to be broken after all.

Chapter 31

Gerard

So, Antoine liked Brooke, and Brooke probably liked Antoine. How was Gerard going to get them to admit their feelings to each other?

More to the point, he thought as he pulled on a clean shirt, why did he even care?

He tossed the dirty shirt into the corner and splashed water over his face, then stared at his dripping reflection. Their coloring was vastly different, but they had the same strong jawline, the same quirk in the eyebrows. Gerard sighed, for despite his jealousy, he had started to develop a bond with his brother. Maybe the connection was because they had shared their mother's womb.

It wasn't that he was ungrateful for the parents who raised him, but he had always longed to know his first ones. Now that he knew about Antoine, his boyhood longings came rushing back. Gerard wanted to know him too.

Maybe he would help Bella play matchmaker with Antoine and Brooke and break the curse. Maybe he could make up for all the time he and his brother had lost.

Elayne would have wanted him to help Antoine.

All through dinner that evening, Gerard struggled between jealousy over others' happiness and the desire to be the man Elayne could be proud of if she were alive. Should he play matchmaker, or leave it all up to Bella?

Bella, however, seemed to be determined to be matchmaker whether Gerard participated or not. "I'm glad Brooke is now eating with us," she announced after the soup was removed. "It is so much easier to discuss things as humans. Talking to her as a candle holder isn't quite the same."

Antoine nodded. "I agree."

Brooke blushed.

Gerard saw the wheels spinning in Bella's expression. He was going to enjoy his dinner and observe how she was going to get Antoine to agree to a ball.

Bella eyed the dining room and asked, "How does this mansion go from looking uninhabited and dusty to clean and cared for so quickly every night?"

"It is part of the curse Aerowyn put on the plantation. We don't know the magic behind it, but we've talked about it before." Antoine looked over at Brooke. "Brooke had a brilliant theory about it that I think makes the most sense."

"What's that?" Bella asked.

Brooke set down her fork. "I think Aerowyn knew it would be a while before the curse was broken—"

"If it ever would be," Antoine mumbled.

Brooke's face dropped. "Don't say that. The hex on this estate will be vanquished completely—I know it." She leaned over and touched Antoine's arm. "Aerowyn didn't have as much faith in you as I do. I suspect she allowed this plantation to look abandoned whenever we're in our other forms. I believe it was for when we stayed objects permanently."

Bella frowned. "I don't see how that helps you at all."

Brooke sipped from her crystal goblet. "If the house stayed pristine, no one would believe it was abandoned. How could an abandoned home be clean?"

Antoine added. "Despite Aerowyn's cruelty, it seems she gave us extra magic to help everything return to the state it was in before the spell. Therefore, the servants have less work to maintain order each night when they're human."

"Is that why Mrs. Watson and her staff get the meals prepared so quickly?" Bella asked.

"Yes, but plus we have a lot of servants," Brooke explained.

"Since things will be simpler with all that help," Bella said slowly, a huge smile creeping over her face, "I think we should throw a ball!"

Antoine choked on a swallow of water, and while Brooke patted his back, he managed, "What?"

"Well," Bella said matter-of-factly, "it would be a perfect way for you to meet a girl to break the curse."

Gerard groaned. Bella was going to make a mess of this.

"If this plantation is going to continue to be prosperous, we need to reach out to other plantation owners. You've been too isolated. Maybe the rich farmers in this area could help us find servants, too. We could call it an early birthday ball. Of course, we would have it in the evening, while everyone is still human."

Bella chimed in, "Gerard and I discussed this earlier, and I think that it is a lovely idea! I miss balls. Not that you would have me participate, but even if I could watch all the lovely gowns from afar, that would be delightful."

"You and Brooke must join the ball," Gerard said in an effort to make it sound natural. "Antoine and I need dance partners until we find eligible women to woo."

"I don't know. It seems too risky." Antoine folded his hands. "We've remained isolated for a reason. What if we change before the party is over?"

"Yes," Brooke interjected. Her brows furrowed. "We purposely have nothing to do with other people in New Orleans or the outlying plantations. We can't let them know our secret! You already know that the hours we remain human are never exactly the same. What happens if Antoine changes into a wolf? He may get hurt—or worse, killed. You know you could have killed him, Gerard."

A chill swept over Gerard at the statement.

"But he didn't." Antoine smiled warmly at his brother. "He was only trying to protect Bella and the estate. Anyway, I have to stay alive to break the curse so Brooke isn't stuck in it forever."

His brother's forgiveness melted that cold place inside, though it didn't drive it away. Still, Gerard glanced between Antoine and Brooke. Maybe Brooke did care for Antoine as much as he did for her. Perhaps the ball was the only way to get them to confess their true feelings.

"No one is going to see Antoine as a wolf." Bella stated with confidence. "We'll make sure the ball guests leave before then. Antoine could meet his true love in the process, and the hex will be broken before he changes into the beast."

Maybe the comment Bella made about Antoine meeting his true love would push Brooke to admit her genuine feelings. Brooke seemed to be mulling over the possibility. She didn't look happy.

"Brooke, you are the estate manager. How soon can we make it happen?" Gerard asked.

"Within a few days, I think," she said hesitantly. "We can send out the invitations and get all the planning done."

"Does that mean we could have the ball in a week?" Antoine slightly smiled as he fidgeted with his hands.

"Yes, which leaves one more week before your birthday." Brooke stood up. "I need to get started now."

Bella bounced out of her chair. "What can I do to help?"

Antoine met Gerard's eyes over the almost empty dinner dishes. "What just happened?"

"You're having a ball, whether you like it or not. You'll find your true love."

Antoine huffed.

"Meanwhile," Gerard said, "I'm having extra dessert."

Chapter 32

Bellarose

T hus began the planning of the ball. Mrs. Watson was brought in to discuss food, and the other servants were brought in to consult about decorations and music. At the time of the enchantment, Antoine had been preparing to throw a party, so a group of disgruntled musicians had been hexed as their own instruments when they weren't in human form.

The servants gossiped unendingly about the decision, eager to break the spell and regain their old lives.

The next morning, Bella cornered Gerard. "You've got to come with me."

Gerard followed Bella outside. "Why did you bring me way out here in a gardening shed?" Gerard's arms wound tightly against his chest. "It's cold today!"

Bella tapped her foot. "I didn't think a little cold would bother Mister Tough War Hero. Anyway, I wanted to be far from listening ears, which means this shed, not the barn and definitely not the house."

"Why do we need to be away from the others?"

"I need you to help me do something."

"If it means we can go back inside, I'm listening."

She rolled her eyes. "After I brought up having the ball, it became more evident that Brooke cares for Antoine. I made the comment about him meeting his true love to see how Brooke would react."

"I caught that. You were a little obvious."

Bella crinkled her nose. "The point is, we need to get them dancing. That is the best place for people to fall in love—like in the fairy tales."

Gerard chuckled. "Fairy tales aren't real. The authors probably have no idea what an authentic relationship between a man and a woman looks like."

"And you're the expert on relationships?" Bella looked him up and down. "How do *you* suggest we get those two to admit their feelings for each other?"

"Antoine admitted to me that he loved Brook, but it will take more than a fancy ball to break the curse."

"He did?" Bella's eyes brightened. "Now they need to admit it to each other. Oh, I know a dance won't break the curse, but Brooke will be dressed in an irresistible gown. She won't look like the house manager—she'll be the princess looking for her prince." Bella stared off into the distance, watching the scene unfold in her mind. "If Brooke looks above her station, she may be open to a relationship with Antoine. Clothing doesn't fix everything, but I'll make sure her hair and dress are perfect for the ball to boost her confidence."

Gerard begrudgingly admitted, "I suppose it could work. A dance may push them into admitting that they're falling in love with each other."

"Listen to you being romantic." Bella beamed at him. "Gerard, you surprise me!"

Gerard smiled widely. "Don't get used to it. I'm still the egotistical toad you abhor."

She laughed, but then bit her lower lip. Bella whispered, "Do you think I could invite Quinn to the dance?"

"Yes, but don't treat me like the plague because you like him more than you like me." He flashed a toothy grin. "Also, don't get distracted from our main duty, which is to get Antoine and Brooke together. When they're in each other's arms, the music should put them in the mood for amour."

Bella gaped. "Gerard, I will never look at you the same. You surprise me a second time, and I didn't think that was possible."

Gerard shifted his weight. "It's a plan, then. You get Brooke into a stunning gown and I'll get my brother to risk telling her how he feels. The rest will be up to them."

"This is going to be wonderful!" Bella exclaimed. "It will be one for the books."

"I hope so."

She patted his arm. "Don't worry. Everything will be fine."

· · — ❋ — · · ·

Bella was ecstatic. It was the first time in an extremely long year that she had something to look forward to. Brooke, Mrs. Watson, and Bella wrote meticulous invitations in fine calligraphy that needed to be delivered to the guests as early as possible. They sent Gerard to hand deliver the missives and collect any extra ingredients from town.

"Since we only have a short time to entertain and feed the guests while we're human, we'll have Creole shrimp cocktail, crawfish étouffée, oysters, beignets, and bread pudding. These all can be eaten standing up to avoid a formal sit-down dinner." Mrs. Watson said. Her voice sounded strange coming from the stovetop. Guests can eat and drink when they're not dancing. It may be out-of-the-ordinary, but they'll only think we're eccentric, which I suppose we are."

Brooke's candlesticks moved in a nodding motion. "I agree. No one in New Orleans has met us. The fact that we've been isolated for so long already feeds into the rumors about the de la Rose family being peculiar."

"Can anything be prepared in advance?" Bella's mind raced. "My parents' parties took weeks of planning, and the cooks prepared several days prior to the feast. The Rose Manor staff doesn't have the time."

Mrs. Watson's smile made the bricks look crooked. "Due to the ball's uncustomary hour, many will have eaten before they arrive. Plus, women don't want to look undainty with a lot of food consumption during a fancy occasion." She clicked her stone tongue. "We should serve pastries, fruits, and cheese, and those will be readied before-hand."

Brooke's gold face scrunched in concentration. "I agree. I've helped with many New Orleans parties before being hired by the de la Roses."

Another thought struck, and a sliver of panic stabbed at Bella. "What if you all don't become humans by the time the party starts? What should Gerard and I do? What if the place doesn't clean itself again?"

"The Hors d'oeuvres will be ready," Brooke said calmly. "You and Gerard only need to set them out before the guests arrive. If they come before we transform, that can occupy them. And all the hexed staff will be out of the ballroom until they become human. You and Gerard can help move those who don't have the ability of scooting themselves."

Brooke's brows weren't noticeable on the gold until they knitted together. "People will expect strange things from us. Our party will be gossiped about for years, but it will be memorable."

Bella gusted a sigh. "Then, that is it. The only thing left to do is find you and me dresses!"

"Well," Brooke added, a sly smile stretching over her face, "I believe you need to go to town and extend one more invitation."

Bella's stomach felt like butterflies were fluttering to escape.

* · ● ☀ ● · *

Bella and Gerard spent the next few hours harvesting roses from his mother's gardens. Whether due to Louisiana's mild autumn or magic, the roses were still in full bloom, and the mansion smelled heavenly. Gerard, however, was grouchy by the time they had finished, and when Bella asked him to saddle a horse for her, he stomped off to the stables in a foul mood. Bella surveyed the buckets and buckets of roses, hoping that magic would keep the garlands fresh.

Her last task done, Bella made herself tidy and tucked Quinn's invitation into her pocket. Her shawl had been ruined when she and Gerard had tried to treat Antoine the wolf, so she pulled a fresh one from the wardrobe. Emma said she looked pretty, and Bella hoped Quinn would think so too.

Gerard helped her onto the horse, warned her to be back well before sunset and to avoid any wolves, then stormed off. She turned the horse toward town, her thoughts on Quinn. She knew he wouldn't accept the invitation if it came from anyone but her. The ride to town seemed longer than usual, but she wended her way through the streets to the smithy behind The Swan.

"Hello, Quinn," she called. When he raised his head, butterflies fluttered in her stomach. Quinn was as handsome as Gerard or Antoine. "How is your day?"

His warm, brown eyes met hers, and he smiled. The kindness of his demeanor wrapped her in comfort. "My day is going splendidly now that you're here. I'll be with you in a few minutes."

He took an arched piece of metal from the fire with long handled tongs, then pounded and shaped it on the anvil. Once it became a horseshoe, he glanced up and back.

He smiled widely, but wouldn't meet her eyes. "I wasn't expecting to see you today. You were here yesterday to pick up supplies."

"I came to invite you to a rather unconventional party." Her voice squeaked a little. "As I explained to you before, Masters Gerard and Antoine aren't ordinary plantation owners. Remember how I told you Gerard was stolen from his aristocratic parents in France and inherited half of Rose Manor when both the Count and Countess de la Rose died?"

Quinn nodded.

"Their birthday is coming up, and they're hosting a ball to celebrate. They're also using it to introduce Gerard as a de la Rose since no one knew that until now." Bella twisted her hair around her index finger. She was babbling but couldn't seem to stop. "Of course, many already know of him from his war exploits, but not his family. Since the mourning period is over, Antoine and Gerard want to meet other plantation owners and townsfolk."

"That makes sense," Quinn said.

Bella swallowed hard and held out the fancy invitation she'd personally handwritten. "Since I'm more a guest than a servant at Rose Manor, they said I could invite anyone I wanted to attend."

Quinn looked at the paper in between her fingers, wiped his dirty hands on his tough apron, and gently took it from her. "You're inviting me?"

"Yes, if you don't mind being my special guest." She bit her lip, then rushed on, "I know you're not used to crowds, but I want you there. You're the only person I truly feel like I can be myself around."

He opened the seal and read the contents. "You wrote this. For me." She nodded.

A faint blush tinged his cheeks. "I would be honored to attend. I... I'll get some nice clothes made." He smiled. "I'm not a great dancer, Bella, but I'll stand by your side proudly."

Bella neared Quinn and squeezed his hand. She didn't care if that was too forward of her. Quinn had made her the happiest girl alive.

"Thank you," she whispered.

"You're welcome." He returned her squeeze. "I've got to get back to work, though."

"Of course," she said.

As she made her way home, the memory of his smile and his hand in hers made the trip go much faster than the one to town. And the thought of Quinn, handsome in a formal attire and—

Her dress! She needed a dress!

Bella almost reined in the horse when the thought struck that Mrs. Watson had put her in the room with the armoire filled with dresses. She would wear the pink one she envisioned dancing in when Emma, the canopy frame laughed at her that first day. She forced herself to focus on Brooke. The house manager needed to look like a princess—overwhelmingly beautiful enough to encourage Antoine to admit his true feelings. Thankfully, the countess had wardrobes full of never worn gowns and underskirts.

Gerard was waiting for her at the stable. He shooed her into the mansion, saying that he'd take care of the horse and its tack. In that moment, Bella caught a glimpse of the kind boy he must have been on the farm. He had stopped treating Bella like the girls who served him drinks at The Swan, and she found him much easier to talk to, although he still had his fits of sullens and moments of hubris.

Bella trotted into the house before the sun neared the horizon. She had three more wardrobes to search through to find the perfect dress for Brooke. Eyeing the cobwebs, she reflected on the first day she attempted to clean the whole mansion. Thankfully, she didn't have to waste time making everything pristine for the guests.

She paused on the stairs. A year ago, Bella had been a sophisticated baron's daughter, and Gerard was a farm boy. A year ago, she wouldn't have met Quinn. She hated to admit that her father's criminal behavior was what brought her to live in America, but it had changed her life in many ways. If it hadn't been for her father's behavior, her path and Quinn's would have never crossed.

Only a year. It was strange how one's perspective could be altered in such a short amount of time.

Chapter 33

Gerard

Rose Manor was a buzz of nervous energy as the ball neared. Things had to go on without a hitch to prevent their curse from being revealed to New Orleans. Though, Gerard had confidence their thoughtful plans would work, Bella's optimism that the ball would be the catalyst to break the spell hadn't rubbed off on Gerard quite yet. The morning of the ball, Gerard suggested they take a walk, and when she agreed, he led her to the gardening shed near the rose bushes.

"What if the hex doesn't get broken?" Gerard raked his fingers through his hair. "Brooke and Antoine may like each other, but is it enough to make everyone permanently human?"

Bella nodded. "I think it is." She paused, then said sagely, "I wouldn't expect you to understand how these things work."

A flash of temper made Gerard frown. "Why do you say that?"

"Because you don't read. Books explain how this situation will turn out." The lines on her face softened. "I know you don't want to admit that someone broke your heart, but I believe you know that love powerful enough to break a spell can exist in the real world."

He stiffened. "You think you have me all figured out, but you don't. Stop trying."

"You didn't deny I was right." Her green-eyed gaze was disconcerting.

Gerard glared back in silence. A new anger boiled to the surface. They had finally gotten past constantly antagonizing each other, but whenever Bella made assumptions about him, it rubbed him the wrong way. For several minutes, they faced each other, and neither one was willing to blink first. Gerard finally moved his eyes and Bella pivoted to leave. He stomped off to brood alone in the barn.

What did Bella know about heart break? Her parents had died, but that is a different kind of love. He'd lost his soulmate, the person he wanted to live the rest of his life with and Bella didn't have real-life experience with that kind of pain.

He kicked the side of the horse stall, and the startled mare whinnied. Gerard hated the inner battle he was having. He absentmindedly picked up a pitchfork and mucked out an empty pen.

Bella might have been correct about losing his true love, but what she didn't know was that he meant to guard his own heart from that kind of loss happening again. He dumped large pieces of manure and soiled straw into a nearby waste bucket. Then replaced the soiled bedding with clean straw.

Neither Bella nor Antoine knew the kind of loss he had experienced. They couldn't understand completely why he was hesitant to trust in love ever again. Gerard begrudged that Antoine may have his happy ending after only suffering a little as a part-time wolf. He cared for his brother, but sometimes he just wanted someone else to understand through their own experience what he battled inwardly on a daily basis.

Bella was right that he had known a powerful enough love to break a curse, but was it better to have loved and lost or not to have loved at all? Giving into darkness and pain was easier, but was it better for him in the long run?

If Aerowyn had truly visited him as a warning the day he shot Antoine near the forest, he was tempting fate with his resentment and anger. If the enchantress was only a day terror, he still needed to get a grip on what he wanted and who he wanted to become.

Every night since he'd seen her at the forest's edge, he had dreamt about her. Each nightmare ended with the enchantress in the middle of a pile of bleeding dead soldiers he had killed.

Gerard scrubbed his hand over his face. If only those gruesome visions would end. If running away from Louisiana and his brother guaranteed they stopped haunting him, Gerard would leave immediately, though having the wealth to do what he wanted, to be who he wanted. What if his demons followed him no matter what he chose to do?

Based on the sun's position, Antoine would be joining him soon, and Gerard wanted to talk with his brother without listening ears. He set the pitchfork down and sat on a bench to wait for Antoine to appear. He'd don the clothes he'd placed outside the barn away from prying eyes. When the quiet shuffle of someone getting dressed sounded, Gerard stood and made his way around the barn.

Antoine spotted Gerard. "Why are you here?"

"I needed to talk to you without Bella or Brooke around."

"What's bothering you?" Antoine pulled his shirt over his head. "You look worried. Do you think I'll fail?"

Gerard rubbed the back of his neck. "I don't know if you'll fail. You care for Brooke, right?"

"Yes, I love her." Antoine's face brightened, but then he shrugged his shoulders. "But does she care enough for me?"

Gerard crossed his arms over his chest. "Bella thinks she does. Look, Antoine, you must clearly tell her how you feel, but I don't know if it will break the spell. Bella's basing her confidence on fairy tales she's read."

Antoine's forehead wrinkled. "You're not evoking a lot of confidence in me. Do you care one way or the other?"

Did Antoine see his mixed-up emotions as Bella had? He thought he was better at hiding what he truly felt.

"If I'm honest, I don't know if I care." Gerard checked over his shoulder. "Because you're my brother, I want what's best for you, but we didn't grow up together. I'm jealous that I missed out on so much." He moved to sit down on a bale of hay and rested his elbows on his knees. "The faint memories that sneaked past the curse aren't the best. Yet, deep inside, I feel this bond for you that only blood brothers can have."

Antoine tucked in his shirt, then sat next to Gerard. "I appreciate your honesty. If I'm to be truthful, I probably have similar memories, except in some ways I think I loved you more than you loved me." He snorted. "That is, if a spoiled three-year-old can love anyone but himself."

"Love is tricky. In that little kid, egocentric way, I loved you too, but now I feel guilty for being jealous of you."

They sat in silence as the last color fled the sky, leaving it dark with only stars for light.

Antoine's left knee bobbed up and down. "Could you promise me one thing?"

Gerard turned to face his brother. "What?"

The dark circles underneath Antoine's eyes were more prominent. "If I become a wolf permanently, will you kill me?"

His request was a gut punch.

Gerard gulped hard before the words, "I can't make that promise," squeezed from his lips.

"You tried to kill me when you thought I was a dangerous wolf." Antoine rubbed his neck. "This would be for mercy. I don't want to live as an animal forever."

It was one thing to be jealous of Antoine, and possibly even to wish the curse would never be broken, but to cause his brother's death was unfathomable. Gerard could only stare.

"I believe—I hope—my death will break the spell for everyone on the plantation. Aerowyn didn't say that it would, but if her goal was to help me learn to be good, or to punish me for being wicked, well... I don't think it is fair for everyone to suffer because of me." He bowed his head. "I would kill myself if I could, but once I turn into the beast, I usually lose the ability to think clearly."

"Antoine, I..." No, he couldn't promise that. It was one thing to shoot a dangerous creature, but now that he knew? Gerard jumped to his feet and patted Antoine's shoulder.

"Brother, you're too serious. Brooke loves you. You both will confess your feelings, kiss, break the curse, get married, and have lots of babies."

Antoine stood up slowly. "Well then, we better get to the house. I'm starving."

"Me too." Gerard rubbed his stomach. "Let's eat before your—our—guests arrive."

They walked quietly toward the mansion.

Gerard's mind was a mess, but he knew beyond doubt he couldn't kill his brother no matter what the outcome.

· · ● ☀ ● · ·

Gerard and Antoine went inside and changed into the finest garments that could be purchased in all of New Orleans. Gerard studied his reflection and gave a nod of approval. He looked like a true prince. When he met his brother at the bottom of the stairs, Antoine did as well.

They waited for Bella and Brooke in the ballroom as guests trickled in. Antoine bowed and over and over again confirmed the rumors Bella had spread about the strange woman who had kidnapped Gerard as a child and how the count had finally found him. Gossip spread as the guests began dancing or lingering over refreshments.

Gerard glanced at the clock on a side table. The young women were late.

Antoine shifted his weight and rubbed his hands together anxiously, then leaned over and whispered, "I don't know if I will be able to tell her."

Gerard slapped his brother on the back. "You will, unless you'd rather be a mangy wolf the rest of your life."

Antoine paled.

Music filled the beautifully decorated ballroom, and an atmosphere of love drifted in the air. As if the grief was new, Gerard's heart ached at the thought of Elayne. For the briefest of moments, anger tinted his vision. It wasn't fair. Antoine had all this, and once he talked to Brooke, he would have the woman he loved.

Then Brooke and Bella entered the ballroom. Their natural exquisiteness was only enhanced by the gowns that complimented every feature. Brooke's red gown with the golden rose embellishments gave her the appearance she was the Lady of Rose Manor. Her dark-brown hair and milky complexion complimented the bold colors, while Bella's light pink dress accented her green eyes and light-brown hair.

Gerard hated to admit it, but both young women were visions of beauty. Of course, he'd noticed Bella the first time he saw her, but her caustic behavior turned off any possible feelings of adoration. She had mellowed, and now he could appreciate her attractiveness while only caring for her as a sister. Nothing more.

The room silenced briefly, and then a buzz of questions competed with the instruments.

"Who are those ladies?"

"Are they princesses from another country?"

"Are they here for the twins?"

Several violins and the harpsichord prompted a few couples onto the ballroom floor. A few men gazed approvingly and made their way toward them, perhaps to ask for a dance.

Gerard elbowed his brother. "Go, before that dance is taken."

Antoine straightened his waistcoat. "Right."

Evidently summoning all his courage, Antoine stepped forward and asked Brooke to dance.

Gerard glanced around. Bella had talked about inviting Gustave's son, Quinn to the ball, and Gerard found him easily enough. Even in his green doublet and black breeches, which Gerard assumed were custom-made to fit around his humped back, Quinn didn't blend in. Several guests sneered in his direction, but the innkeeper's son didn't seem to notice. His attention was fixed on Bella.

It was curious that she was attracted to someone from that class. She came from aristocracy, a world of shallow opinions, and Quinn would never be considered desirable marriage material. As Gerard was watching, though, her green eyes found Quinn, and he witnessed Bella brighten.

Jealousy washed over Gerard as Bella ignored the well-dressed guests and made her way to the stableboy-turned-blacksmith. It doubled when Antoine joined hands with Brooke in his dance. Bella and that puny specimen of a man, then Antoine and his estate manager? It wasn't fair.

Gerard had wanted his brother to find true love, but that spike of envy made him want Antoine to know the pain of separation and poverty too. He knew he could easily ruin this moment for his brother.

The supposed-enchantress's warning ran through his memory: Actions would have consequences.

The minuet ended. Several guests spoke to him, and a few hopeful mothers introduced daughters, but Gerard only watched Brooke and Antoine as they tried out the English country dance and the cotillion. The couple stared at each other even when they exchanged partners as they moved across the floor. It was the epitome of two people falling in love. That was how Elayne had looked at him. Other men tried to get Brooke's attention, but in Antoine's presence, they quickly lost their courage at the last minute.

Antoine was going to get what he desired before the evening was over, which was the reason Bella suggested the ball. Gerard had helped, so why was seeing his brother's bliss grating on his nerves?

Bitterness brewed. Aerowyn forced him to grow up in poverty while Antoine had his heart's desire. He had literally fought and killed to help his family. Antoine had everything handed to him. Gerard had ached—still ached—over Elayne's death.

His fists curled.

When Antoine left Brooke's side to get some refreshments, Gerard gave in.

"Brooke, I no longer can restrain myself." His eyes roamed over her body. "You are too beautiful to leave alone. May I have the next dance?"

"Uh, y-yes?" Brooke stammered.

The music began, and, throwing a look of triumph at his brother, Gerard slid Brooke's arm into his. Antoine set the small plates aside and pushed his way through the crowd toward them.

"Well, Brooke, I'm not sure if you've given much thought to what you will do when the curse is broken." Gerard walked her to the dance floor. "If my brother manages to get someone to fall in love with him tonight, maybe you and I could have a casual dalliance? Mind, I don't plan on ever getting married. A girl in your position could do worse."

Brooke turned several shades of red and came to a stop.

"I-I- think you have the wrong idea of me. I may only be a servant, but I'm—"

"Not available!" Antoine roughly pushed Gerard away from Brooke. Anger and betrayal darkened his face. "Brother, what are you doing?"

A lump formed in Gerard's throat, but shame was a weakling's move. "I wanted to have some female companionship. It's been too long since I've had any, and let's face it, Brother, you don't deserve someone as lovely as Brooke." Gerard's lips curled. "I'm the one who suffered in the past. It's my turn for happiness."

Antoine features turned rigid. "I know I don't deserve any of this, but I thought you were on my side. We may not have grown up together, but we're family. I love—"

Light brightened the window as the sun appeared below the horizon—as if lifted by an invisible force. The hands on the large standing gold clock spun rapidly around its face.

"Antoine," Brooke cried.

Everyone stopped, every eye turned to Gerard and Antoine, and the room fell deathly silent. Gerard's ever-changing emotions landed on shame and regret—he was a better man. He needed to make this right before it was too late.

Chapter 34

Antoine

Antoine's bones snapped as his body twisted abnormally. Clothes ripped. Arms and legs stretched and twisted while hands and feet became paws. His nose and mouth lengthened into a wolf's snout. Skin stretched and prickled as fur grew from his pores. The wild nature of the wolf emerged immediately. Predatorial instincts overpowered human ones.

He lost every ounce of civil cognizance as the caged animal expanded into being, growling and huffing.

Wolf crouched, ready to pounce.

Antoine was swallowed by the beast, and—no one was safe.

Chapter 35

Brooke

S uddenly, screams filled the room

Horrified, Brooke could only watch as the guest backed away, their cries of terror echoing back at them. Antoine, the man she truly loved, was inside the beast, but his eyes showed no sign of his true self. Only an animal stared back. She reached for him, but in the blink of an eye, she shifted into the golden candelabra.

Brooke was safe from Antoine, but the guests were not.

She wanted to scream, "Someone get him outside," but this time, even her ability to speak was gone. She scanned the room, searching for someone who would help, someone who would understand. The other servants, however had changed too, though none of the guests noticed.

All eyes were on the ferocious wolf.

Not caring for her own safety, Bella approached Antoine, her hands with palms up. "It'll be alright," she said in a soothing tone. "Calm down."

Instead of pacifying the wolf, his hackles rose at her voice. He crouched, his long fangs exposed in a snarl.

"Bella, no!" Quinn shoved himself forward, whipping out his sword as he moved.

The beast lunged.

Chapter 36

Bellarose

S avage eyes, wicked teeth, and long claws reached for Bella, but Quinn was faster.

He slashed the blade across the creature's side, and the wolf dropped onto the polished wooden floor.

"What have you done?" Gerard shoved Quinn aside and kneeled beside the whining beast. Blood puddled around the wolf as he labored to breathe.

A sob racked in Bella's chest. "Quinn, please put your sword down and help me."

Quinn's brows furrowed, but he set down the weapon as she had asked. "Be careful Bella. He may still be able to hurt you."

Gerard stripped off the elaborate, fitted coat and wadded it against Antoine's side.

Noises reverberated in Bella's ears.

"Bella."

She looked up to see Quinn in front of her, but her tears blurred his face.

"Bella," he said again, softly, "how did that creature get in here?"

"No!" Gerard exclaimed. "Look at me. Don't go to sleep. You can't!"

Quinn darted a look at the wolf. Bella did, as well. His eyes were closing. His breathing grew erratic. His chest moved slower with each passing second. Bella's hand covered her mouth. Antoine was going to die.

"You can't go to sleep. I just—I just found you." Gerard lifted the wolf's giant head to his lap, and blood darkened his blue waistcoat and breeches.

Bella touched the wolf's ruff, then looked up at Gerard. His forehead wrinkled in grief and fear.

Antoine grunted in pain, and Gerard gasped in unison.

The ringing in Bella's ears subsided enough to realize that the guests' screams had stopped.

She turned toward Quinn. "Quinn, I..." Tears dashed from her cheeks. "You..."

He dropped to his knees beside her. "There's magic here I don't understand, isn't there?"

She nodded.

"I'm sorry. I didn't know."

"You had no way of knowing. You were trying to protect me."

Brooke's candelabra form lay on its side nearby. Gerard was sobbing into the wolf's fur. There was no one else, so Bella stood.

"I am sorry for the dramatic stop to the festivities," she said clearly, "but I think it is best if you all go home." She looked down at Antoine and then added, "Although, if anyone knows how to treat an injured dog, please stay and help."

No one did.

Quinn aided Bella with escorting the curious spectators to exit. He returned with her while she sat motionless—helpless—at Gerard's side, waiting for Antoine's demise.

"I can help your dog."

Bella's attention snapped to a darkened corner of the room.

A raven-haired woman with a lavender gown emerged from the shadow. "I can help your dog," she repeated. The stranger's melodic voice and warm, chocolate eyes unnaturally calmed Bella's anguish. "Let me see his wounds."

Gerard had become eerily quiet. His tear-stained face revealed obvious turmoil. Setting his brother's wolfish head carefully on the floor, he stood to block the woman from Antoine.

"Please trust me." The words came out gently. "Gerard, I can help."

A spark of hope lit in Bella's heart. "If she can save Antoine, you need to move."

He shifted in a semi-trance while the woman bent over the wolf and removed Gerard's blood-soaked coat. She sang in an unknown language, and the wolf remained completely still.

The charm wore off and Gerard exploded into anger. "What are you doing, Witch? Help him—he's dying!"

"My dear Gerard, my song is helping him, but only you can truly break your brother's curse."

A memory from long ago—from a book?

Golden hair that sparkled as diamond dust could transform into rich chestnut brown and then to raven locks in the blink of an eye.

Bella sprang to her feet. "You're Aerowyn!"

The enchantress smiled softly. "Yes, and I'm here to finish what I started."

Gerard asked savagely, "What exactly does that mean?"

"I'm here to give you a chance." Aerowyn's eyes turned blue and her hair became golden blonde.

Gerard's jaw tightened. "Me? What do you mean?"

"My song has already started to knit his wound together. The blood loss weakened him, but Antoine is alive. Yet, is he really living when he must be a wolf?" Aerowyn sang one more line of the strange sounding melody and then faced Bella, Quinn, and Gerard.

"Antoine would rather be dead than apart from the woman he loves." The enchantress gave the candelabra an empathetic smile and returned her scrutinizing gaze toward Gerard. "If you choose to take his place, you will become my loyal companion as a wolf. You will break the spell, and all the enchanted beings in this house will return to their normal forms permanently."

Bella gasped, and Quinn placed a strong hand on her arm.

Aerowyn held her hand to her chest. "Do you love your brother enough to do this?"

To give up his life and freedom to serve the enchantress who had ripped him from his family?

Bella couldn't fathom such a sacrifice.

Chapter 37

Gerard

I t was the enchantress from his nightmares.

There was no doubt.

She was exacting punishment on him for killing so many soldiers after he lost Elayne. For treating others with contempt. For his absolute selfishness. With her powers, she probably also knew how many times he wished for Antoine's hex to be permanent.

He had already lost too much and he couldn't lose his brother. Not now. He'd known it the moment Antoine had asked Gerard to kill him if he became the wolf permanently. He didn't want his brother dead.

Could he give up his humanity to save his brother? Would breaking his brother's hex be better than giving into the darkness? Would his inner wounds finally heal if he exchanged his life for Antoine's?

The petty moment of selfishness had spiraled into something unimaginable. No, he couldn't have Elayne back, but at least Antoine could have Brooke.

This was the sacrificial love Aerowyn had been searching for all along.

Bella shoved between him and the enchantress. "How dare you manipulate other's lives like this? Haven't you done enough to this family?" Her hands clenched. "These brothers have been separated too long. And now you want to take them away from each other—forever? You could heal him. I know you could."

For once, her argumentative words almost summoned a smile. Gerard forced himself to say, "I'm surprised you care, Miss Bonnay."

Her green eyes were even greener from tears. "Of course I care, you exasperating oaf!" But her voice broke. "Gerard..."

The enchantress remained silent.

Gerard focused on the motionless wolf-form of his brother. No, at that moment, he couldn't deny his love for Antoine.

He turned to Bella. "Could you please make sure my family in France is taken care of?"

"You can't go through with this."

"After all this time, you finally care about me." He blinked rapidly. He wouldn't show weakness. Not now. "Well, you're too late. Besides, that Quinn fellow seems to be smitten with you."

Apparently nonplussed by the supernatural turn of events, Quinn put an arm around Bella's shoulders, and she leaned against him.

Bella drew a deep, shuddering breath. "If that is what you truly want, Gerard, I will see it done."

Gerard turned to the candelabra. "Brooke, take good care of my brother. He loves you and will eventually be able to tell you that. I'm sorry. I shouldn't have let my petty jealousy interfere with your happiness. And Brooke? Don't let your past roles determine your future ones."

Aerowyn pulled out a golden wand topped with a sun-shaped design. "It's time, Gerard."

Gerard's muscles and bones strained and broke, reforming in such hideous ways that a howl of pain was force from his throat. Before he lost human consciousness, he saw Antoine transform into a man, alive and breathing. Brooke was at his side, pulling a table-cloth over his naked form.

They would have their happy ever after.

That was enough.

Chapter 38

Aerowyn

The ballroom vanished with a scent of sulfur. She would revisit New Orleans soon to deal with another unsavory fellow, but for now, she'd return home with her new companion. She and the large black wolf materialized on a clifftop covered in emerald four-leaf clover. Gerard sucked in a huge breath as he gazed over the magical azure sea crashing against the rocks below.

"This is my people's island," she said. "My home, Sans Âge Isle, the Without Age or Ageless Isle. It is where my kind live. I call myself an enchantress, but I'm really fae."

She knelt down and met his stare with her own, "Now what am I going to do with you?"

Gerard whined. *I'm not a wild, untamed beast like Antoine became. I understand you.*

"Yes." Aerowyn pierced his thoughts with her own. *We can communicate mentally through our bond. You have been given the ability through my magic. In time, I will teach you how to block any thoughts you don't want me to hear.*

Why did I have to become a wolf? Gerard asked at once. *You saw my willingness to sacrifice myself for my brother. Wasn't that enough?*

She frowned. *Magic has a price. I can't cast curses on people and then reverse them whenever someone asks me to. Once I set the spell in action, the only way to break it has to be a sacrifice. Your willingness wasn't enough—you had to sacrifice your humanity by becoming a wolf.*

Gerard chuffed out a wolfish snort. *How many of your kind manipulate humans' lives?*

I cannot say. Her eyes changed hues.

Cannot or will not? Gerard growled

"Let's go home." With her melodic voice, she had supernatural power to alter Gerard's mood slightly without his awareness he was being influenced.

Aerowyn led Gerard away from the cliffs and into a nearby forest full of lush greens and browns. The scents of rich soil and vegetation filled the air, and she drew a deep breath, reveling in the familiar touch of other-worldliness and indefinable magic. They walked rather than evaporated home so Aerowyn could pull out the isle's soothing qualities and continue her control over Gerard's anger.

When they reached a waterfall, Aerowyn drew in the calming elements. Gerard's tumultuous thoughts weren't completely gone. He was understandably angry over the turn of events. She buried deep the doubts she had over her own actions. The curses had to be making a difference or what was she doing?

The colorful flowers that surrounded the turquoise liquid of the falls shimmered like diamonds in the sun. Basking upon a large rock in the middle of a lagoon was a group of beautiful mermaids, whose long flowing hair covered their chests.

The serenity of the lagoon distracted Gerard from his anxiousness and he asked her, *Are those real gemstones cascading down alongside the water? And mermaids? Bella told me about them once.* He glanced up at Aerowyn, *But mermaids don't exist.*

"Yes, to all your questions," she said.

They strolled beyond the lagoon through fields of spices and herbs that humans valued for wealth. She could sense Gerard's confusion as new odors, sounds, and sights overloaded his senses. It took a little bit of her own magic and the island's extraordinary features, but Gerard became more composed the closer they got to her home.

The journey finally ended in her forest where towering trees shimmered with an array of red, purple, orange, pink, and blue leaves. Gerard followed her to a giant, blue tree with a stairway leading to a matching door that opened into the trunk. She held the door open, and Gerard padded in. He paused a moment, then walked wearily to the plush cushion she had provided.

You knew, then. You knew I wouldn't let my brother die, he thought, but she didn't answer. He turned three times, then settled on the soft mattress and yawned noisily. *Why would any of your people want to leave this paradise?*

"It's a long story," she said sorrowfully.

I'm obviously not going anywhere. You might as well tell me.

She quickly changed her visage into the girl, Elayne.

He growled. *Stop It.*

She shook her head. "This is a dim version of my true form. I never let humans know what I look like, but you're no longer a man." Aerowyn motioned at herself. "This is a dulled aspect of the real me."

His ears went back. *You were Elayne?*

"I was Elayne, and yes, I'm still alive."

Echoes of his thoughts drifted into her mind. Anger at being deceived, sorrow at the loss of Elayne, and love he had for Elayne bled through his reflections.

She winced.

You look like the girl I loved, but that was a lie. You pretended to be Elayne. The ugly image of an evil enchantress who cursed people into misery overlaid his thoughts of the young woman he loved.

She interrupted his inner battle. "No. I'm not really Elayne."

You tricked me. I... He grunted. *Blasted mind reading! I know you aren't—you're the evil enchantress.*

Aerowyn sighed. "I'm not that either, but it is hard to explain."

Gerard rested his head onto his paws. She felt the tension radiating from him. All her magical ways to relax him couldn't erase the betrayal he experienced. She sensed Gerard was fighting for self-control. He had let that slip this evening, and he was determined not to allow that to happen again.

As I said, I'm not going anywhere—because I can't—so go ahead and try to explain to me who you are. Why do you hex people?

"My kind used to live in a land that bordered the humans. We had magic and immortality, but there was one beast that could kill us. We stayed in our world where we were protected from the only monster that would harm us." She moved to sit on a chair that faced Gerard's bed. "Some grew discontented with perfect lives and looked for adventure in reckless ways. King Peter of the Fae forbade us to go into the land of the humans to keep us safe, but his own daughter didn't like rules."

This sounds like that book Bella carried around with her.

Aerowyn nodded. "Yes, *The Scorned Fae.*"

Bella eventually told me the story, after she forgave me for taking the book from her the first day we met.

"That book was written about King Peter's daughter." Out of thin-air a clear glass of golden liquid appeared in Aerowyn's hands, and she took a sip.

Which character was the king's daughter?

"The one who died from the dragon's fire."

Oh—so that's the one creature that can kill you?

Aerowyn took another sip. "Yes. Her selfishness devastated her father. After her death, he was inconsolable." She placed the glass down
and rubbed her eyes. "The king used powerful magic to move all the
fae to this island and bound us to it. He wanted us as far from dragons
as possible, but he also wanted none of us to repeat her mistake."
Aerowyn lifted the gold tear-drop shaped pendant. "This necklace
keeps me tied to Ageless Isle forever."

Gerard cocked his head. *Elayne wore it.*

"Yes," she said.

What would happen if you stopped wearing the pendant?

"I would surrender all my magic and immortality." She twirled the
pendant between her fingers. "I will never take it off unless I'm ready
to give up those things. King Peter, the most powerful of all the fae,
gave his people the choice to serve his purposes, or leave Ageless Isle
permanently and become human. His goals, however, reach beyond
that."

What exactly are King Peter's goals?

"He wants the fae to rid the world of selfishness, greed, and cruelty."

Gerard woofed. *Oh, is that all? Why doesn't he move a few moun-
tains while he's at it?*

"Magic makes success easier, but it doesn't always work." She
rubbed her temples. "Your parents never learned; that's why your
brother and his household were cursed. You had to relearn the lesson
after you thought I was dead. You have a good heart, but you allowed
circumstances to make you boorish and self-absorbed."

Gerard sat up. *You broke my heart!*

"It was a test, and you failed it. There are all kinds of broken hearts in the world." She sighed. "You may have been the key to breaking your brother's enchantment, but there are lessons you still need to learn."

Does that mean I can be freed from this form eventually?

"It is possible."

How?

"You aren't ready to know yet."

Gerard absorbed her words and then finally asked the question that had been hovering in his mind from the moment he'd seen her true form, *When you pretended to be Elayne, was it all a lie—the part about loving me?*

"I played a horrible trick on you, but I couldn't reverse your brother's curse without your help. When I read your thoughts about how you wanted to marry me and take me home to France, I knew you wouldn't be able to help your brother if I was in the way."

Gerard narrowed wolfish eyes at her. *You didn't answer my question.*

Aerowyn knelt beside him and rested a hand on his strong shoulder. "All you need to know for now is that you're immortal, and I'm immortal. We will have our happily ever after—eventually."

Chapter 39

Bellarose

T he scent of sulfur filled the room. Bella blinked away hot tears as the vision of Gerard transforming into a large black wolf evaporated into mist with Aerowyn. The ballroom was a scurry of motion as those who were no longer cursed hugged and cheered over their freedom.

Quinn removed his arm from around her shoulder and bent to pick up his discarded sword. His face was loaded with questions.

"I never told you before, but there's no hiding it now." Bella faced Quinn. "Rose Manor was cursed by Aerowyn, the enchantress, who just disappeared with Gerard."

Antoine's voice was shaky as he asked, "What did Gerard do?"

"Your brother became the sacrifice needed to break the curse." Brooke sat near him on the ground.

Antoine stood slowly, careful to remain wrapped by the tablecloth. "But why did Aerowyn take him away and turn him into a... wolf? Did you see him transform? I think I did, but it wasn't registering as my own body was morphing." Antoine paled.

Brooke nodded. "I think everyone in this room did, but our transitions from object to human was easier than yours." Brooke gingerly stood pulling her full gown up so she wouldn't stand on it. "Aerowyn claimed Gerard needed to switch places with you in order to save your life, and as the only way to break the enchantment on all of us."

Antoine's eyes locked on Brooke. Bella felt a tumult of emotions. When she glanced over at Quinn, he looked concerned for her. Were her feelings displayed all over her face? On one hand, Quinn's protective chivalry brought her bliss that turned to despondency when she thought about being homeless again. If Quinn ever cared for her, it wouldn't matter if she was forced to leave New Orleans in search of a different home. She didn't know if Gerard's twist of fate changed her future at Rose Manor.

Mrs. Watson approached. "Monsieur Antoine, is it all right to dismiss the musicians and others who were not house staff before the curse?"

Behind them a group had gathered of several people. Antoine turned and addressed them.

"You are all welcome to go home and if you need any assistance, financial or other caused by your imprisonment here, please don't hesitate to ask." He pulled the cloth tighter to him. "I know my apologies could never give you back all the time lost, but I'm truly sorry for all you've had to go through this past year."

Antoine's throat bobbed. Brooke edged near him with knitted brows.

The gatherers dispersed as Rose Manor staff returned to their duties before they were abruptly transformed into objects and the musicians were given carriages to return to their homes. Bella wondered how they would explain their long absence.

Antoine then turned to Brooke. "I have something I want to ask you, but I planned on looking more— um— put together when I did it." He slightly bowed. "If you'll wait for me here, I'll return as quickly as I can."

Brooke's eyes followed Antoine's exit until Quinn asked, "Is it too prying to ask why this place was cursed?"

Bella quickly responded. "Maybe I can tell you some other time."

She wanted to unload all her burdens on Quinn as the sensation of upheaval reappeared as it had when she had lost her parents. A tightness in her chest caused her to panic.

"Is something wrong?" Quinn gently held her hand.

"When I discovered Gerard was master of this estate, I almost left the first day I arrived, but he told me he needed me as a maid. We soon thereafter found the plantation was cursed and didn't need a housekeeper, but I stayed to figure out how to help since they didn't remain human long enough during the day." Her eyes brimmed with tears. "I no longer have a purpose to be here and I don't have any place to live."

Quinn rubbed her hand with his fingers. "I could see if my dad would allow you to return to the tavern as a bar maid." Then he shook his head. "No, that's a bad idea."

"Bella, you can stay here. We can use your help now that we don't have magic to keep the estate in order. I'm sure there is something you can do." Brooke placed a hand on Bella's shoulder.

"I know exactly what Bella can do for us." Antoine interrupted as he entered the ballroom.

Bella wondered how he got dressed so fast, but he probably had his butler help him. Antoine wore a new suit that made him look just as princely as the one that tore when he had become a wolf. The red doublet, gold vest, and black breeches complimented Brooke's ballgown perfectly.

Antoine knelt on one knee in front of Brooke. "I must tell you that I love you before another enchantress decides to curse us. Would you do me the honor of marrying me?"

Brooke's wide smile made her face glow. "Yes, I'll marry you, because I love you too."

He stood and pulled her into his embrace and they kissed. Bella couldn't contain her happiness for them and she briefly whispered, "Finally." The servants who had remained to tidy up after the ball, stopped and clapped.

Quinn's face reddened, but he leaned into Bella, still holding her hand. Immediately she felt conscientious as her heart beat like hummingbird wings. Was he going to kiss her?

Antoine exclaimed, "Bella, please will you help us plan our wedding?"

"Yes, Bella, I will need your advice on everything!" Brooke beamed.

If there was going to be a kiss, the moment had passed as Quinn pulled away. He smiled shyly. "I guess you still have a purpose to be here for which I'm glad. I need to get back to town, but I hope to see you again under less exhilarating circumstances."

"Yes, I would like that." Bella didn't want him to go, but she understood.

Perhaps Bella did have purpose after all, but as she watched Quinn drive away in the carriage, flashes of pages from a book quickly darted in her mind's eye. She pushed them away, because for the first time, she was seeing an actual happily-ever-after come true—except for Gerard. What would happen to him as he lived out his life as a wolf with an enchantress?

Bella felt a spooky sense this wasn't the last she would see of Aerowyn or Gerard. Again, a strange vision of a book—this time it was oversized—drew her inside it. She blinked rapidly and it disappeared. She explained the illusion away as her strong desire for her own storybook ending. Deep in her heart, Bella saw the possibility and leaned on that hope.

Letter & About Author

Dear Book Dragon,

Thank you for joining me on this journey. Since you've reached this part, you can see that this new twist on "Beauty and the Beast" is not finished. The next adventure, "Bellarose and the Pirate", introduces the infamous Captain Jasper Falcon—another retelling, this time featuring a character with a hook for a hand. If you enjoyed this book, please rate, review, and tell anyone you can about my stories.

Always Imagining, Carla

ABOUT

Carla Reighard lives with her husband and three cats, Han, Leia, and Kylo, who all attempt to "help" when she's crafting a new saga. Fairies, mermaids, talking animals, and supernatural bicycles were her childhood companions, but until the publication of *Elle's Magical Shoes*, they remained inside her head. If you're bold enough to read fairy tales and brave enough to believe in redemption, you've found the right book. See more of her work at https://carlareighard.com.

instagram.com/carlareighard/

goodreads.com/author/show/7085189.Carla_Reighard

facebook.com/people/Carla-Reighard/61567154826280/